DATE DUE			

F
DON

Donnelly, Elfie.

4299

Offbeat friends.

**CREEKSIDE ELEMENTARY SCHOOL
MORENO VALLEY CA**

Offbeat Friends

ALSO BY ELFIE DONNELLY

So long, Grandpa

Offbeat Friends

ELFIE DONNELLY

TRANSLATED FROM THE GERMAN
by Anthea Bell

CROWN PUBLISHERS, INC.
New York

Originally published in German as *Der rote Strumpf*
Copyright © 1979 by Cecilie Dressler Verlag, Hamburg
English translation copyright © 1982 by Andersen Press Limited
First American edition 1982 by Crown Publishers, Inc.
Originally published in the English language in 1982 by
Andersen Press Limited in association with Hutchinson Limited,
3 Fitzroy Square, London W1.
Manufactured in the United States of America
Published simultaneously in Canada by General Publishing Company Limited
10 9 8 7 6 5 4 3 2 1

The text of this book is set in 12 pt. Electra

Library of Congress Cataloging in Publication Data
Donnelly, Elfie.
Offbeat friends.
Translation of: Der rote Strumpf.
Summary: A Viennese grade-schooler catches her parents
off-guard when she smuggles an elderly mental patient
whom she met in the park into their home.
[1. Mentally handicapped—Fiction.
2. Family life—Fiction]   I. Title.
PZ7.D71930f 1982   [Fic]   82-7995
ISBN 0-517-54617-5   AACR2

For Janne/Jacob,
whichever he prefers.
And, of course, for Stoffi
and Peter too.

Offbeat Friends

1

SHE had been looking for a coincidence. Mari was always looking for coincidences. Without any coincidences or things happening by chance, she got bored at home in the afternoons when both her parents were out.

It was at least three weeks since the last coincidence, as Mari could tell from a glance at her Coincidence Book. She had started the Coincidence Book on the first of January last year. It had four columns to a page: one for Lucky Coincidences, one for Unaccountable Coincidences, one for Silly Coincidences, and one—the narrowest column—for Unlucky Coincidences.

The column for Unlucky Coincidences contained her last entry, dated September 7.

Blue Volkswagen ran down child. Child: Anni Wegenstein. Lives on Nissel Street. I know child. Driver of car: Richard Wegenstein!!!! Anni's father!!!!! Anni slightly injured by own father.

But there had been no coincidences since Anni Wegen-stein's accident. Why not? That couldn't be a coincidence. Mari wondered whether to enter "September 30, no coinci-dence yet" in the column for Unaccountable Coincidences, which was still empty. She decided not to. Well, it was high time for another coincidence. Nothing interesting had hap-pened for weeks and weeks, just boring everyday stuff like going to school, doing lessons, coming home, having lunch, feeling cross, doing homework, playing, going to bed.

Thursday seemed endless. Mari had walked along Cumber-land Street toward the church. She was going to sit on the bench that one of the savings banks had put opposite Beserl Park, for old people to watch the children playing soccer. However, there weren't many old people in the neighbor-hood who were interested in children playing soccer, so the bench was usually empty. Not everybody wants a soccer ball kicked at his head.

Mari thought it was odd that there were always more children than usual chasing around Beserl Park and playing soccer on Thursdays. Last autumn she had gone from pri-mary to secondary school, which meant going to school a different way, so she didn't know many of the children in the park. She was familiar with some of them by sight, though, and she could make a good guess at what classes they were in at which schools.

Mari sat down on the bench. Fat Hansi came around the corner. Mari folded her hands, pursed up her mouth in a silent whistle and looked up at the branches above her. She hoped Hansi wouldn't notice her. He sat behind her at school, and she couldn't stand him. He had bad breath and he was ugly. Mari did not like ugly people. Sometimes she didn't like herself either, though she was not sure if she was ugly or not. She changed her mind on the subject at least twice a day. She had straight brown hair that was short in front but long at the back, with bangs across her forehead. Ordinary blue eyes. No long, silky eyelashes like Rosemarie Schredl. No uptilted nose like Susi Pomberger. Ordinary mouth. Mari was rather short for someone of eleven. In between fat and thin, but certainly nowhere as fat and ugly as Hansi!

Fat Hansi didn't notice Mari. He leaned against a tree and tried to dig his hands into his trouser pockets, which he found he was unable to do, because he was wearing the stupid pair that had no pockets. Hansi wanted to be friends with tall Norbert. Whenever Norbert shouted, "Go away, Fatty!" Hansi smiled broadly but stood his ground. He never even squealed when the soccer ball landed in the pit of his fat stomach. Mari felt a certain sneaking admiration for Hansi and the toughness of his stomach.

Someone coughed. Until now, Mari had not noticed that another bench had recently been put outside the church. This bench was occupied. There was an old woman sitting there; she was the person who had coughed.

Mari was about to look away and go on watching fat Hansi and tall Norbert, because some sort of coincidence might happen, when suddenly the sun came out. The sun had been behind clouds all day, and now that it began to shine, it shone right on the old woman's feet. Mari had to look twice to make sure she had seen right: yes, the old woman was wearing odd stockings.

The right one was bright red. The left one was black. Mari's attention wandered from the red stocking for a moment, but when she looked back at the old woman's feet again, they were the same as before. She was still wearing stockings that didn't match.

Mari was still looking from the red stocking to the black

stocking and back again when the old woman said, "My right foot gets so cold, that's why."

"What?" Mari heard herself ask.

"Red is warmer," said the old woman.

"Yes, of course," Mari said.

Mari often said "Yes, of course" without thinking, as she had just done. Why, no, she thought. No, what nonsense! How could it be warmer?

The old woman said no more. Mari began to feel scared. Perhaps it was a magic stocking that could hypnotize her. She suspected it might be, because she found her eyes drawn to it again. The stocking fascinated her. The longer she looked at it—it was a knitted woollen stocking in plain stocking stitch—the more reasonable it seemed that it would keep the old woman warmer than the black stocking on her other foot.

People all ought to wear red stockings or socks, especially in winter. Mari decided to suggest it at school. No, at home first. Mother was always going on about her cold feet. Father used to say no wonder: Mother wore such thin nylon tights it wouldn't be surprising if her toes eventually froze right off. But Mother just shrugged her shoulders and went on moaning about her cold feet.

"Red is much prettier than black," said Mari out loud.

"And warmer. That's what matters," said the old woman on the bench.

"Prettier," said Mari. "Well, maybe warmer too."

Mari looked more closely at the old woman. First her eyes. Mother said a person's eyes could tell you what he was really like. If so, the woman on the bench must be nice, because she had nice eyes. She also had a tartan skirt.

She could have done better with a different pullover. Her mauve pullover clashed with the blue and green tartan skirt. It was V-necked, and you could see another sweater underneath it. Mari wondered if the old woman was wearing more layers of sweaters under that. She looked old, Mari could see that. Granny was old too, but Granny was old in a different way. Somehow or other Granny seemed even older than old. Mari wondered why.

"How old *are* you?" Mari asked, and she immediately wished the words were back in her mouth and then back in her head, where they had come from. Father had told her that you never ask a lady her age.

Too late: the woman had heard the question.

"Old," she said. "Very old. I've been around forever." She got up and sat next to Mari. "For ever and ever. For seventy-eight years."

Mari moved a little farther away as the woman moved a little closer to her.

"My granny is three years younger than you," she said, thinking that the old woman's hair could do with brushing and combing; it looked very tangled. But Mari knew that combing out the tangles would hurt. Tears came into her own eyes every morning when Mother brushed her long hair at the back.

"I'm a granny too," said the old woman. "And I have grandchildren."

"Do you?" said Mari, stupidly. She didn't know what else to talk to this funny old lady about, but she thought she was nice and somehow—well, somehow interesting. Different, like a coincidence. Perhaps this old lady means something special to me, Mari thought. Yes, I'm sure she does! This feeling got stronger, but all the same Mari felt the old woman was a little weird. Not as weird as Mrs. Übersoll from the first floor of their apartment building, who had runny eyes and a bad-tempered dog, but weird all the same.

Should she get up and go home now? Mari didn't like to be rude, and if the coincidence of meeting this old lady should turn out to be important, it would be silly to go home. The old woman was really nice, only so funny. . . .

"How many?" Mari asked, to keep the conversation going. The old woman didn't seem to mind the silence, but Mari did. She felt uncomfortable when conversations just died away. "How many grandchildren, I mean," she explained.

"I don't know," said the old woman.

Well, *that* got Mari nowhere. "I don't come here very often," Mari said, changing the subject. At the same time she began to fish for something in her pocket. She arched her back, braced her feet against the ground, grunted and produced two jelly beans. She put them in the hollow of her hand and held them out to the old woman, who didn't say thank you, but took the green one.

How rude! thought Mari. As if people offered her green jelly beans every day of the week. And even if they did, not by someone who loved jelly beans as much as Mari, especially green ones.

But the old woman ate the jelly bean with such pleasure that Mari felt it almost made up for her sacrifice. She gobbled jelly beans herself, but this old lady chewed and sucked the jelly bean, then she smacked her lips and finally sighed happily. She's a dear, thought Mari. "My name is Mari," she said.

"And mine is Maria," said the old woman, who was not just an old woman now: she was Maria. "Maria Panacek."

"That's almost the same as Mari, only a bit longer," said Mari. "I'm really called Marianne—on my birth certificate, I mean. But everyone thinks Marianne is too long, so I've been called Mari ever since I was tiny."

"Mm," said Maria Panacek. "I am called after the Mother of God. She's my godmother."

"Who? The Virgin Mary?" Mari wrinkled her brow, puzzled.

[6]

"Yes, yes, the Mother of God," said Mrs. Panacek, and she stood up so suddenly that her shoes threw up a cloud of dust that tickled Mari's nose. Mari felt her eyes water. She was on the point of sneezing but couldn't quite manage it. It was something that happened to her often.

"Where are you going, Mrs. Panacek?" asked Mari, getting up and following her.

Mrs. Panacek was not listening, which annoyed Mari. She walked along beside the old woman.

"I must get my chocolate," said Mrs. Panacek. She was heading for Embacher's Delicatessen, opposite the church.

"Can I come with you?" asked Mari, but she didn't really expect an answer from this peculiar old lady so she began counting the last few coins in her purse. Could she afford a bag of jelly beans or not? Yes, she could.

Mari had never been in a shop with anyone who ignored her as much as Mrs. Panacek did. The moment she was inside the shop Mrs. Panacek went over to the display of chocolate, took a bar of nut chocolate costing eight Austrian schillings off the shelf, and tucked it carefully into the waistband of her skirt—"You're supposed to take a basket, Mrs. Panacek," said Mari—after which Mrs. Panacek walked right past the cashier and straight out into the street again.

"Good-bye, Mrs. Panacek," said the cashier, a red-cheeked girl, in friendly tones.

"Hey!" Mari's jaw dropped open as she stood there by the checkout counter. Stunned, she put her jelly beans on the moving belt and stared at Mrs. Panacek as if she were seeing ghosts.

"Four schillings," the cashier told Mari. Mari paid. "Don't you feel well?" the girl asked her.

"I'm okay," gasped Mari, casting an anxious glance at Mrs. Panacek, who was standing just outside the door happily unwrapping her stolen chocolate. Then Mari looked at the cashier. She didn't look all *that* stupid; she must have noticed!

Seeing Mari's face, the girl began to laugh. "Came in with Mrs. Panacek, did you?"

"Yes."

"I don't suppose you've known her long?"

"Only an hour or so."

"Yes, that's what I thought."

A customer came up to pay, and the girl put out her arm and gently moved Mari aside. Mrs. Maria Panacek was still standing outside the shop, firmly planted on the spot and eating her stolen goods.

"Run along, then," the cashier said to Mari. "You can see she's waiting for you. That'll be one hundred and ten schillings thirty, please," she told the customer.

Rata-tat-tat went the cash register: *ting!*

The girl gave the customer some change, put her coffee in a paper bag, wrapped her bottle of cooking oil in a piece of old newspaper, and put the bread rolls into her old leather shopping bag.

"But she *stole* that chocolate!" said Mari very quietly.

"No, she didn't," said the girl. "Mrs. Panacek comes from Alder Yard."

As if that explained anything! What sort of place was Alder Yard? And what did Alder Yard have to do with a stolen chocolate bar? Mari didn't understand the cashier at all. Normally she'd come down hard on shoplifters, and there was a huge sign in the shop, saying:

SHOPLIFTERS WILL BE HANDED OVER TO THE POLICE.
WE ALWAYS PROSECUTE.

But the cashier showed no signs of calling the police.

The customer lifted her heavy shopping bag off the counter. "The loony bin," she grunted, as Mari politely held the door open for her. "That old woman's from the loony bin."

"It's not a loony bin, it's a mental hospital," said the cashier to the customer, shaking her head. And she added, to Mari, "Mrs. Panacek's quite harmless. Wouldn't hurt a fly. She's only a bit mad."

"How do you mean, mad?"

"Well, crazy! I mean, she's not quite normal. She comes in here every day for a bar of chocolate, and the people who run the Alder Yard Home pay us at the end of the month."

"You mean she really does live in a lunatic asylum?" asked Mari, as she watched Mrs. Panacek outside the door. Mrs. Panacek was rolling the wrapping paper from her chocolate bar into two small balls: one of the colored paper, the other of the silver foil. The cashier didn't answer; she was already ringing up the next customer's basket of shopping. Mari pressed her nose to the glass and went on watching Mrs. Panacek.

She doesn't *look* like somebody out of a loony bin, thought Mari. Yes, and if she *is* out of a loony bin, all full of crazy people, what's she doing here in the street? I mean, they're all locked up! Has she run away, or what?

Mari couldn't make it out. But as standing about in the shop was getting her nowhere, and as Mrs. Panacek, outside the shop, was looking at her little balls of chocolate paper in a perfectly amiable way, Mari finally went out. It's not true, she thought. The cashier was just teasing me. Yes, I bet that's it. On the other hand, Mrs. Panacek really had stolen something. And stealing's a crime, right?

Then she was beside Mrs. Panacek again. Looking sideways at her, suspiciously.

"*I* am allowed to!" said Mrs. Panacek proudly.

"Allowed to steal chocolate?"

"I'm allowed to. You see, I'm crazy."

"My father says I'm crazy, too," said Mari, suddenly feeling very relieved, though just why she didn't know.

"I'm crazy, and you're crazy," said Mrs. Panacek. "Well, now I'm going back to the loony bin."

And she went away.

Mari stayed put, as if rooted to the ground. She watched Maria Panacek walk away in her tartan skirt, her mauve pullover, and her odd stockings, one red and one black, getting smaller and smaller, and turn the corner of Cumberland Street, where the choirboys used to lean their bikes up against the church wall.

Mari walked slowly home.

2

"*LA TIENDA*—the shop. *Inaugurado*—opened. *La es-clava*—the slave girl; *la hija*—the daughter . . . put the kettle on for coffee, Mari. *Excusare*—to apologize . . ."

Mother was muttering her Spanish vocabulary, leafing through the book and pacing up and down the kitchen. Mari too muttered, "The daughter, the slave girl," as she filled the kettle with cold water.

"No, use hot water," said Mother. "*Compre*—I bought; *ayer*—yesterday . . ."

Mari poured the cold water down the sink, turned on the hot water and refilled the kettle.

"Enough to make one crazy," Father said crossly.

"What? What's enough to make one crazy?" Mother lowered her book, but her eyes were still fixed on an imaginary Spanish word somewhere on the white wall.

"You pacing up and down. Enough to make anyone

crazy," said Father. He added, "I'll have some coffee too, please."

"*La ganga*—the bargain," murmured Mother, as she obligingly sat down at the kitchen table, casually swiping off a few crumbs left over from the last meal as she did so.

Mari didn't like to see Mother sweeping the crumbs straight on to the newly swept floor. Suppose *she* did it!

"I'm starting work on a new film," said Father, picking at the new scab on the cut on his finger.

"Don't do that," said Mother sharply.

Mari gave Father a little slap on the hand. She went over to the cupboard, stood on tiptoe and got down the coffee, opened a new packet of filters and waited for the kettle to begin singing. Or rather whistling, not just singing. Water for coffee must be boiling hot; warm water won't do. Mari had learned to make coffee from Granny.

Mother finally put her Spanish book away. She would have liked to go on learning Spanish vocabulary, but when Father began talking about a new film you couldn't concentrate on anything else. Mother had long since given up the attempt to change her husband. She had tried for many years, and it was no good.

"Ow!" squealed Mari. A drop of boiling water fell on her knee. She gritted her teeth.

To hear Father talk, thought Mari, you might take him for someone really big in films: a film star or a director. But he was only a property man. When the film script said: "The genuine Chinese vase crashes to the ground. Paling, Amelia stares at it," it was Father's job to find the genuine Chinese vase. Of course it was not really genuine Chinese, only a vase that looked as if it might be genuine. A genuine Chinese vase would be far too valuable to be broken on television.

Apparently Father was at work on the props for a new

film, set in the nineteenth century. Father loved the nineteenth century, especially nineteenth-century props.

Mari put the cups on the table and received a grateful
glance from Father. He even stopped talking about the
film. "That's my girl," he said, putting his arm around
Mari's waist. She didn't like it, and slipped out of his grasp.
It made her giggle when he did that, because it reminded
her of love films. But you can't play a love scene with your
own father. She supposed you might with that good-looking
boy Gusti in seventh grade, only he was stuck-up, and he'd
think Mari was too short for a love scene.

That was Mari's great sorrow in life: her height.

She just did not, would not grow. In between her tenth
and eleventh birthdays she had grown exactly half an inch,
hardly even worth mentioning.

And when she looked hard at Father, she realized he was
to blame for her failure to grow. Father was only five feet
three inches tall. For a grown man, Mari thought, that was
almost lilliputian. Mother was five feet three inches too, but
it was different for a woman. So Mother said. And she was
right; she looked to be a perfectly normal height.

For years and years Father hadn't liked Mother to wear
high-heeled shoes—until he got the idea of doing the same.
Since then (and anyway it was fashionable just now) Father
had worn shoes with heels at least two inches high, although
it meant he had to take great care his trousers were long
enough to cover them. He didn't want people noticing his
heels; it made him feel self-conscious.

Mother and Father were enjoying their coffee. Pleased,
Mari sat down on the empty wooden chair, feeling quietly
happy. It was nice at home today.

In fact, Mari felt absolutely fine until Mother asked, in a
very worried tone, "Aren't you feeling well, Mari? You look
terribly pale." And at that very moment Mari did feel her-

self turning pale, because if somebody asks if you aren't feeling well, you can easily start imagining yourself ill until you actually are ill.

"No," she said belligerently. "I'm perfectly okay, Mother."

"You don't eat enough," said Mother. "I mean, here are Father and I sitting drinking coffee, eating Aunt Trude's apricot cake, and you aren't touching it. You left half your lunch today, too."

"Well, I'm not hungry," said Mari, who didn't want to say she had eaten a whole bag of jelly beans. Mother was in mortal terror of gum disease and periodontitis, and spent a fortune on assorted brands of antidecay toothpaste and antigum-disease mouthwash. Not to mention a new toothbrush every week. . . .

Perhaps it was because Mari had her mind on this subject that Mother said, "We've got an appointment with Mr. Steinlechner at two-thirty tomorrow, about your brace."

Mari hated to think of it: an instrument of torture worn in the mouths of at least five children in her class, and now she was going to have one, because her front teeth didn't point forward, but inward and backward instead. "It's quite lucky one of my own fillings came out yesterday," said Mother.

"That's right; two birds with one stone," grunted Father, bending to pick up the spoon he had dropped.

"Mother," said Mari, "is a red stocking warmer than a black one?"

Mother shook her head, puzzled. It gave her a little double chin.

"What?" asked Father. He shook his own head; he couldn't see what Mari was getting at. "What do you mean?"

Mari herself realized the question sounded funny, and

she stared hard at the kitchen floor as she repeated, doggedly, "I asked if a red stocking can be warmer than a black one."

Father, who often read books and magazines about the way to bring up children, tried to look patient. Mari could see him trying to act in the psychologically correct manner.

"Why, of *course* a red stocking can be warmer than a black one, Mari dear!" said Father. "Always supposing the red stocking is made of something warm, like good thick wool, for instance, and the black one is made of, well, let's say of ordinary . . . ordinary . . . er—" Father looked around for help.

"Cotton." Mother took pity on him. "Cotton, or that kind of thing."

"Yes, cotton, or that kind of thing," repeated Father, relieved.

"Oh," said Mari blankly.

"Yes, you see?" Father nodded.

Mother shook her head again. "I wonder what makes you ask, Mari," she said. It was more of a statement than a question: Mother liked to give herself her own answers. In this case, her answer to herself would be: well, Mari's capable of anything.

"Because of the woman," said Mari. "And both stockings were made of wool."

"What woman?"

"The woman in the park."

Mother gestured helplessly.

"The woman in the park!" Mari repeated. "There was a woman there who had one black stocking and one red one."

"An old woman, was she?" asked Father.

"Yes," said Mari. "Well, sort of old."

"She'll have laid her hands on odd stockings when she got dressed in the morning, that's all," said Mother, shrugging her shoulders. As she noisily cleared the coffee things into the sink, she added, "I hope I don't get absentminded like that when I'm old."

"No, she says the red stocking is warmer than the black one," said Mari.

Father picked up the newspaper, a sign that he had lost interest in the conversation. "The old girl's probably crazy," he said.

"Isn't there such a thing as color temperature?" asked Mother, raising her voice so as to be heard above the hot water she was running to rinse the cups.

"Yes," Father said from behind his paper, "but that's different." When Father saw that Mother was washing dishes, he liked to hide behind the newspaper. In theory, he thought he could wash dishes just as well, but in practice, he thought, well, Mother had more experience washing dishes and so on.

Mother said if he had a guilty conscience about it, that was progress at least.

"Color temperature has nothing to do with how hot or cold your feet feel," added Father, who always thought he knew everything. He lowered his screen of newspaper, and then he didn't just hear Mother washing the dishes, he could see her at it too, which was probably why he swiftly raised the paper again. "Your old lady was probably crazy," he repeated.

"Yes, actually she *is* crazy," said Mari. "She can even help herself to chocolate in a shop and nobody punishes her."

"Nonsense," said Mother impatiently, picking up the used brown coffee filter in her fingertips and putting it in the trash can, which was full to overflowing anyway. Emptying it was one of the jobs Father had "volunteered" to do.

"No one can just help themselves to chocolate like that," said Father, shaking his head.

Mari was annoyed. Did he think she was thick, or what? "It's true," she said. "Mrs. Panacek really *can* help herself to chocolate. The cashier told me so."

"What cashier?"

"In Embacher's Delicatessen," Mari explained. Father was often slow to get the drift of things.

"Oh?" he said, looking surprised.

"You mean Trude Jelinek?" Mother was rubbing her roughened dishpan hands with handcream for roughened dishpan hands.

"I don't know her name," said Mari, rather crossly. "She's a bit plump. Red cheeks and fair hair."

"Yes, that's Trude Jelinek." Mother nodded. "You mean she lets the customers get away with stealing?"

"Listen, Mari, if you see someone shoplifting you ought to say so," Father told her. Mother looked at him doubtfully.

"Ought to say so!" snapped Mari. "You're just not *listening* to me! Mrs. Panacek *did* steal the chocolate—but it wasn't really stealing, because the people at the Home pay at the end of the month. At least that's what Trude Jelinek says."

Mother gave Father a meaningful look and took a deep breath. "And what's that got to do with the red stocking?" she asked, sitting on the arm of Father's chair and letting him put an arm around her waist.

"The woman who stole the chocolate was wearing odd stockings," muttered Mari. She wished she'd never started telling them about Mrs. Panacek. Why do things get so complicated when they could be so simple? All she had wanted to tell them was that Mrs. Panacek was allowed to steal things and wore odd stockings. Surely you could tell a person that sort of thing without letting yourself in for hours of cross-examination, couldn't you?

Apparently not, because Mother murmured something to the effect that maybe they ought to take her to a child psychiatrist, and Father murmured something else to the effect that she was probably being overworked at school.

And they both looked at Mari the way they looked at the falcons in the zoo at weekends—falcons being one of Mother's hobbies—with clinical interest.

But I'm not a falcon, thought Mari crossly, I'm your daughter. "Oh, forget it," she said. Her chair squeaked on the linoleum as she pushed it back, on her way out of the room.

"Mari!" called Mother. "Wait a minute."

Mari turned around. Unwillingly, but she did turn around.

"This old lady was—was crazy?" asked Mother, guardedly.

"Yes," said Mari. "Well, that's what Trude Jelinek said. So did Mrs. Panacek—*she* said she was crazy."

"Really crazy?" asked Father, dubiously. "A crazy woman allowed out on the loose?"

"Well, she lives in the lunatic asylum," said Mari.

"In a mental hospital?" exclaimed Father. And Mother said, "Oh, come on, you must be wrong! People aren't allowed out of mental hospitals."

"They're allowed out of *that* mental hospital," said Mari. "Mrs. Panacek is anyway."

Mother began talking to herself. "Come to think of it, they did open a new mental hospital a few weeks back. The Alder Yard Home, that's its name. No, wait, it's not exactly new, it's been renovated and reopened with new staff. There was something about it in the local paper—a home for the psychologically disturbed."

"She's not psychologically disturbed, she's crazy!" said Mari, and Father said, "It's the same thing these days."

"Wasn't it always?"

Father shrugged his shoulders.

"I only skimmed through the article," said Mother. "All I remember is that the neighbors kicked up a fuss. They said if the inmates were going to be allowed out no one was safe in their beds. The patients always used to be locked up, but not now, and some of them could be dangerous lunatics, so the neighbors daren't leave their windows open at night anymore."

Mari stood there in the doorway, aware of something brewing up which boded no good. Not to her or to Mrs. Panacek either. The atmosphere in the kitchen was very depressing; Mari didn't know why.

"But Mrs. Panacek is very nice," squeaked Mari, feeling as if she had to defend herself against an invisible attacker. She wanted to hit out, flail at the air with both arms. She'd have liked to wipe out the last quarter of an hour altogether, and then neither Mother nor Father would know a thing about Mrs. Panacek. "She really is, she's very nice," Mari repeated. "And the Home pays for the chocolate, and odd stockings may look funny, but then one of her feet gets so cold."

She could tell that she was only talking herself into trouble. "I mean, *you* sometimes get cold." She appealed to Mother. "You know what having cold feet is like!" Why didn't Mother stop staring at her?

"Your mother always has both feet cold," Father told her. "Having *one* cold foot isn't normal."

"What do you mean by normal?" asked Mother, and she added thoughtfully, looking at her feet, "I do feel the cold a lot."

"Because of your thin nylons," Father pointed out.

Mari turned her eyes heavenward in despair. Father looked at her sternly, and wagged his finger in front of her

nose. "Mari, you're not to talk to people like that, understand? I mean, of course they're human beings the same as
you and me, and of course they have a right to—er—well . . .
but I don't want *you* mixing with people from a mental
home. One never knows—"

"But," said Mother, at rather a loss, "if this woman is
allowed out . . . ?"

"Yes, I don't understand that part of it," admitted
Father.

Mari was now thoroughly confused. She was surprised to
discover that the story of the chocolate and the odd stockings could do such funny things to the atmosphere in the
kitchen, which she could feel was made up of a little fear, a
little annoyance and anger and a great deal of confusion.

But Mrs. Panacek *is* so nice, and so funny, thought Mari
sadly, and she says such amusing things. Mother and Father
ought to be glad another interesting coincidence had finally
come Mari's way.

As her parents were now sitting in silence, and time was
ticking away so loudly, Mari left the kitchen. Father called
out, "Mari, you do know you're not to talk to strangers,
don't you?" From out in the hall, Mari nodded.

3

SCHOOL finished at a quarter to twelve on Friday. The children pushed through the narrow classroom door, all eager to be out first. Except Mari.

Not that she didn't want to get out of school too, but she knew that if she hurried home, Granny would be there. Mari had nothing against Granny, only against Granny's Friday lunch, which was fish, of course.

Mari's grandmother was a woman who did everything the right and proper way, the way it's always been done. Especially when it came to food. She served spinach on Thursdays, fish on Fridays, carp at Christmas time, herring salad on New Year's Eve, lamb at Easter, and made cakes for people's birthdays. Mari didn't mind the birthday cakes at all, because Granny's butter-cream sandwich cakes were excellent, but she hated herring salad and carp.

Mari was the last to leave her desk.

"What's the matter?" Hilde had asked her.

"Nothing," said Mari, "except it's Friday."

"Oh, I see," Hilde had said, nodding sympathetically, because she knew how Mari felt. "Well then, see you." And Hilde went off, because if she didn't get home early enough her mother made a fuss, and she might be deprived of pocket money and television.

Mari left the classroom slowly. Her schoolbag seemed as heavy as lead today.

It was not just Granny's fish: there was also the fact that her parents had quarreled yesterday evening. As usual, no one had told Mari why, which was infuriating, because it made her wonder if the quarrel was her fault. Fish for lunch! If only Granny would at least fry fish sticks, like other grandmothers. But Granny thought fish sticks were common, and she claimed all the protein had been frozen out of the fish, and in any case fish were not rectangular. And that was that.

Granny always served fish that still looked like fish, so on Fridays Mari would find a fish on her plate gazing at her with big sad eyes: Granny didn't chop the fishes' heads off. "The heads are the best part, Mari. Eat up, now! Fish is good for the brain."

And Mari would have to bite back a snotty answer as she got the white flesh of the fish down somehow or other, closing her eyes and thinking of the vanilla cream waiting for her in the fridge, all nice and cool and smooth and creamy colored.

I won't go home today, she thought. Well, not right away. Granny can just wait.

Mari walked down Diesterweg Street.

She stopped at the baker's, which smelled of freshly baked rolls. Mari went in and bought one. It was still warm, and when she bit into it the crust was crisp. There was all the difference in the world between a nice fresh roll and a stinking fish. She took another bite of the roll, and the world looked much rosier.

I wonder what Mrs. Panacek's doing, thought Mari, and then she was tempted to believe she could work magic, because at that very moment a figure that might easily have been Mrs. Panacek came around the corner of the church.

It walked like Mrs. Panacek. Mari had noticed that Mrs. Panacek took little steps as if she were walking a tightrope without any rope.

Mari went down Cumberland Street and right past number 51, where she lived and where Granny cooked fish on Fridays. She was following the little figure at the other end of the street. She caught up with it where Cumberland Street curves around the Catholic church, opposite Beserl Park.

It *was* Mrs. Panacek.

She had just sat down on the bench, and was letting the sun shine on her closed eyelids.

"Hello," panted Mari. She put her case down on the dusty ground.

Mrs. Panacek opened her eyes a crack and closed them again directly. She didn't say "Hello"; she didn't say anything at all. But she smiled.

Mari sat down beside her. She glanced down and to her left to see if Mrs. Panacek was still wearing one red and one black stocking, and was pleased to see that it looked as if Mrs. Panacek's right foot was cold again today.

"What happens when they're both cold?" asked Mari.

Mrs. Panacek did not answer. This time Mari didn't mind. Perhaps Mrs. Panacek didn't feel like answering. Mari wished she could do the same: just not answer if she didn't feel like it, which often happened, especially at school or when Mother was in a bad mood. Or when Granny asked how she was ever going to get big and strong if she didn't have enough sleep, or eat enough animal protein, not to mention minerals and trace elements.

This thought brought Mari back to the fish. Sighing, she

leaned back and stretched out both legs. Now she was sitting just like Mrs. Panacek. Still trying to copy Mrs. Panacek, Mari closed her own eyes, but because it's tricky imitating someone with your eyes closed, she opened them slightly to see if Mrs. Panacek had changed her position.

"I'm hungry," said Mrs. Panacek. "It'll be fish at the Home today."

"Yes, because it's Friday," said Mari. "It's fish at home too."

Mrs. Panacek's eyes flew wide open, and she took Mari's forearm in a firm grip.

"Listen to me! You mustn't eat fish, no, not on any account!" said Mrs. Panacek. Her voice was loud and insistent. She sounded scared.

"That's what I'm always telling Granny," said Mari. "Fish is horrible."

"Never, never, never!" cried Mrs. Panacek. She plunged both hands into her short gray hair and began combing it with her fingers, over and over again. "Fish is poisonous! Fish is poisonous!"

Mari felt helpless. She was not sure what the matter was with Mrs. Panacek. Mari herself certainly didn't like fish, in fact, eating fish made her feel quite sick, but she had never heard anyone say it was poisonous. At the worst, it might be bad to eat if it had gone bad during the long journey from the sea to Vienna, and it wasn't fresh anymore. Yes, that might happen, and food poisoning was supposed to be very nasty, especially fish poisoning. What would you call it if the fish itself ate something that gave it a stomachache? Wasn't that fish poisoning too? When people get a stomachache, why don't we call it people poisoning?

Mrs. Panacek let go of Mari's arm again and leaned back on the bench.

"I own a fishmonger's," she said quietly.

"You do?" asked Mari in surprise.

"But they stole it from me!" said Mrs. Panacek. "They stole it—my son-in-law; my daughter had to marry him, you know—*he* stole my shop! And now he's trying to poison me so I can't tell anyone." She took Mari's arm again. "You have to be careful what you eat," she said, looking earnestly into Mari's eyes. "You have to be very careful. They tried to poison me with a piece of cod, oh, yes, they did, a piece of cod! I sell the finest cod in town, and the carp in my shop are bigger than those at the fishmonger's in Mariahilfer Street too. He's probably hand in glove with the fishmonger in Mariahilfer Street. Oh, yes, I know it's all a plot."

Then Mrs. Panacek looked around, hunching her head between her shoulders. "I must keep calm," she said. "I must keep calm. That doctor, the lady doctor, she says it isn't true, but what does *she* know about it? Her pills won't stop the poisoner and his accomplices. I can't defend myself against them with pills, can I?"

Mari didn't know what to think. She had never heard anyone tell such an awful story, yet she couldn't imagine somebody *really* wanting to harm nice Mrs. Panacek. Why would they? Because of the fishmonger's shop? Had Mrs. Panacek made that up? And Mari was sure Mrs. Panacek had never hurt a soul.

I must find out more about Mrs. Panacek, Mari decided. It might not be a good idea to go on talking to her about fish; fish got her so excited. Mari wondered what other subject of conversation to broach. What would interest Mrs. Panacek?

"My father's working on a new film," said Mari. It was the only thing she could think of at short notice.

Mrs. Panacek did not say anything until Mari had been talking for at least five minutes. Then she said: "They really have old-fashioned costumes like that?"

"Yes," said Mari eagerly. "It's fantastic! They even have suits of armor in the wardrobe. Father took me there twice, and they let me dress up. I went to the carnival in my costume, and naturally it was the best of all, because nearly all the things were real. Well, they *looked* real. I went as a medieval lady, and Miss Hedi—she's a makeup lady, she's a friend of Mother's too—Miss Hedi did my face for me."

"I've got a doll," said Mrs. Panacek. "I've got a doll, and I dress her up in different clothes. A medieval costume would be nice. . . ."

"I've got a doll too," said Mari. "Her name's Anastasia. But I don't play with her anymore, not since Father ran the vacuum cleaner over her in the very middle of the living-room carpet, and there was a crack, and Anastasia's arm was crushed."

"Crushed?" asked Mrs. Panacek, sounding agitated.

"Yes." Mari nodded.

"Then he killed your doll!"

"Dolls are already dead," said Mari. "I mean, they were never alive."

"No, no, no!" cried Mrs. Panacek. "Every doll can be alive if you'll let it. I always let my dolls be alive!"

Mrs. Panacek was sitting on the very edge of the bench, swaying back and forth. She looked as if she were about to stand up.

Mari, who liked a bit of drama, pointed to the left side of her chest with her right hand and said in a loud and very theatrical voice, "Alas, my father has murdered my innocent little doll! Oh, woe is me!"

Mrs. Panacek was not impressed. However, she said, "One day I'll show you my doll." She opened her eyes wide, looking very mysterious. Her voice dropped, and she said intensely, "It's a great honor to be allowed to see my doll." And then Mrs. Panacek closed her eyes.

Mari realized time was running out. When she closed her

own eyes now she seemed to see Granny before her. At this moment Granny would be in the kitchen, with the table set, looking at the time and drumming her fingers impatiently on the table, wondering who to call and who might know where Mari was. She'd wonder whether to call Mother at the office, and then she'd decide to wait a little longer, give herself another hour. She wouldn't want to worry Mother; it was bad enough for herself, Granny, to be worried.

Mari felt sorry for Granny and the fish, cold in its pan on the stove by now. It would smell even worse cold than when it was hot.

She knew she'd have to go home. If she didn't go home now, at once, this minute, there'd be trouble with Granny, and when there was trouble with Granny, it was rapidly followed by trouble with Mother and Father.

Mari was torn between feeling sorry for Granny and wanting to stay with Mrs. Panacek. She liked sitting here on the bench with Mrs. Panacek very much. Sitting on a bench with Granny would not have been the same. Mrs. Panacek's head was full of surprises and interesting oddities. Not everybody's like that, thought Mari. In fact, nobody else Mari knew was like that. Certainly not Granny. There was no room at all for interesting oddities in Granny; there wasn't room inside Granny for anything but tidiness and order, order and tidiness.

If Granny were here now instead of Mrs. Panacek, Mari knew exactly what they'd be discussing: school, and lack of protein, the unhealthy habit of eating sweets, dear Mother who worked so hard and was so lucky to have such a wonderful husband, and the virtue of punctuality, and the disorder inside Mari's head.

They certainly would *not* be discussing: the dangers of poisoned fish, dead dolls, dolls' murderers, medieval ladies, odd stockings.

Mari's schoolbag had fallen over. She fished it out from

under the bench with her foot, put it on her knee, and wiped the leather clean with the sleeve of her sweater. She didn't want to go yet, but she'd go all the same, because she knew she must.

"I'm going now," said Mari reluctantly. "Will you be here again tomorrow?"

"Always," said Mrs. Panacek. "I'm always here when the red has gone out of the sky."

"I see," said Mari. She liked the way Mrs. Panacek had said that. It sounded like poetry.

"Be seeing you then," she said.

Mrs. Panacek turned her head to look at Mari, who was standing in front of her, and smiled a little smile. Then she turned her head away again and stared as if spellbound at the entrance of Embacher's Delicatessen, directly opposite.

"Good-bye."

"Good-bye. See you tomorrow," said Mari, running off. As her feet were taking her in the direction of 51 Cumberland Street, but with her head still turned to look at Mrs. Panacek, she almost collided with Father Klechel, who was just coming out of the church. He smiled kindly at her. He always smiled kindly at children, only he couldn't remember their names because he was very old.

He was still smiling at Mari. " 'Scuse me," she stammered, and ran home.

Breathless, she ran up the stairs of the building. There was a smell of roast pork and sauerkraut on the first floor, and a smell of goulash on the second floor. The third floor smelled of fish, and Mari stopped running. She wrinkled up her nose and put her schoolbag down beside the mangle, which had been there ever since the first tenants moved into the building in 1930. It wasn't used anymore because people don't put their sheets through a mangle these days; they use an electric pressing device instead.

[28]

She couldn't find her key at first. Even when she knelt down on the prickly front doormat to tip out the contents of her bag, and her textbooks and exercise books all fell out on the cold stone floor, she still couldn't find it.

"Marianne!" said Granny, shocked. Mari jumped, and looked up at Granny's face. Granny, eyes flashing as she stood above Mari, said, "The fish is cold now!"

4

"I shall call the police!" shouted the man. "Shoplifting, that's what it is!"

He hooked the thumb of one hand into the pocket of his white overall and waved the other in the air, pointing from the shelves (which looked perfectly normal, stacked in a perfectly normal way with assorted kinds of sweets and chocolate bars) to the notice saying SHOPLIFTERS WILL BE HANDED OVER TO THE POLICE. WE ALWAYS PROSECUTE.

Mari had come in to buy bread for supper, and the moment she got inside the shop she saw: the man who must be new there, shouting his head off; the new, dark-haired cashier, acting as if none of this had anything to do with her and the trembling Mrs. Panacek staring at the red-faced man, wide-eyed, and clutching her chocolate tightly to her breast with both hands.

Standing there beside the new cashier, Mari did not know what to do.

"Looks like a loony," said the new cashier. You could tell from her voice Mrs. Panacek gave her the creeps.

"You just leave Mrs. Panacek alone!" Mari said. She went over to the new man and plucked at the sleeve of his white overall.

"Go away, little girl. Don't interfere," said the man, pushing Mari aside.

"You leave Mrs. Panacek alone!" Mari repeated. Her thoughts were whirling around in her head. "Granny!" she said to Mrs. Panacek, visited by sudden inspiration. "Granny, you forgot your money!"

And Mari produced her own purse and offered it to Mrs. Panacek, who did not take it.

Mrs. Panacek was looking as if none of this concerned her in the least. She was gazing with interest at an orange lying on the floor of the fruit and vegetable section.

"Granny's absentminded," Mari desperately chattered on. "She's always leaving things behind. She left her key in a bus last week, and her umbrella too, even though it was pouring with rain."

The man frowned. "That chocolate costs eight schillings!" he said. "And tell your granny to use a basket next time. That's what they're for!"

Mrs. Panacek balked slightly when Mari urged her toward the cashier. The new man was arranging the rest of the Israeli oranges in between the Granny Smith apples and the lemons, and muttering crossly to himself. Mari cast him another anxious glance, and asked the cashier, "Where's Trude Jelinek? The other cashier, I mean?"

"Gone on vacation," said the new girl. "For three weeks." She tapped two keys on her cash register, and the drawer full of money shot out.

"Who's he?" asked Mari, looking at the man piling up oranges.

"The new branch manager. Eight schillings, please."

Mari got eight schillings out of her purse without taking her eyes off Mrs. Panacek. She wanted to get out of Embacher's Delicatessen as fast as possible, along with Mrs. Panacek and the chocolate. She nearly forgot the bread. She was wondering whether to tell the new cashier about Mrs. Panacek. No, she'd just warn Mrs. Panacek she mustn't take anything from the shop for a while. Not until Trude Jelinek was back from vacation, then she could tell the new manager piling up the oranges about the mental hospital paying the bill once a month.

Then they were out in the street. Mari didn't know just what to say. She opened her mouth and then shut it again once or twice, and popped a couple of jelly beans in when it happened to be open.

"Want a jelly bean?" Mrs. Panacek did not. Shrugging her shoulders, Mari put the jelly beans away again. "Well, I'm going to the dressmaker's," she said. "Nelli Radocha, at 43 Cumberland Street."

Mrs. Panacek did not seem to know the dressmaker, which was amazing; Nelli Radocha was a familiar, not to say a conspicuous figure in this part of town. There were several reasons for this. One: Nelli had bright red hair. Two: Nelli was a good dressmaker, specializing in First Communion suits and white Communion dresses, and three: Nelli was always pregnant. It was the butcher's boy who made up the rhyme:

Here comes Nelli,
With her big fat belly.

At the moment Nelli was expecting her fifth child. "Just like a rabbit," Granny sometimes said, shaking her head in a way that didn't tell you whether she thought well or poorly of rabbits.

[32]

Mrs. Panacek was walking along beside Mari at a comfortable pace. Well then, she'd just have to come to the dressmaker's with her. It seemed that Mrs. Panacek didn't feel like talking today.

But when they reached the shoe shop at the next corner, Mrs. Panacek suddenly turned into the entrance of a building and walked straight through it into the yard behind. Mari ran after her. "Mrs. Panacek, I'm in a hurry," she said. "I was due at Nelli's five minutes ago."

Mrs. Panacek looked at Mari, puzzled, before she said indignantly, "Oh, but we must get rid of the chocolate first!"

She took the chocolate bar out of the waistband of her skirt and held it under Mari's nose. "This is the poisoned chocolate," she solemnly explained. "Anyone can see *that* at a glance!"

All Mari could see was an amiable blue cow on the wrapping paper and the words FULL MILK CHOCOLATE. "It doesn't say anything about being poisoned," said Mari, guardedly.

"They'd never put it in writing!" Laughing, Mrs. Panacek tapped her forehead. "Fancy thinking a silly thing like that!"

"No, of course they wouldn't," said Mari, and Mrs. Panacek said, "Now to dispose of it!" She went over to the nearest of a row of trash cans, and tried to throw the chocolate in, but in spite of her efforts she couldn't get the tight-fitting lid off.

"Here, let me help." Mari helped Mrs. Panacek tug at the lid. It squealed and finally gave way. The chocolate disappeared into the depths of the can, landing with a soft plop among the left-over food from the restaurant's kitchen at the back of the building. Mari looked sadly down into the can. Eight schillings gone west! And she only got ten schillings a week for pocket money. Thank goodness it was Friday today. Mari wondered seriously whether to ask the

Home for her eight schillings back at the end of the month, like Embacher's Delicatessen, but she didn't really think she'd ever dare. Somehow she didn't think it would be right, either.

Mari banged the lid back on. "And now we can go to the dressmaker's!" said Mrs. Panacek happily, patting her on the shoulder.

"You're okay again now, aren't you?" asked Mari.

Mrs. Panacek shouted that she felt so well she could tear a palm tree up by the roots. Her voice, echoing round the yard, was so loud that several windows opened, and curious faces looked out.

"Oh, yes!" cried Mrs. Panacek, cupping her hands around her mouth and shouting through them. "Tried to poison me, didn't you, eh? But I'm clever, too clever for you! I'm not falling into any of your traps!"

The windows closed again, the faces disappeared, and the only sound was the postman clanging letterboxes in the building.

For the second time that day, Mari tugged Mrs. Panacek away by the lapel of her coat.

5

"ONE and a half inches," grunted Nelli, leaning a hand on the edge of the table as she hauled herself up from her knees. "Haven't grown much, have you?"

Nelli hung her tape measure back around her neck and then put her hands to the swollen, pregnant stomach under her smock. Mari stared at that stomach, fascinated, wondering why it didn't burst like a balloon.

"Shut up!" Nelli shouted across the kitchen at the bedroom door, but little Schurli went on yelling.

"Perhaps he's hungry, Nelli," Mari suggested, feeling a bit intimidated. She always felt that way at Nelli's because four very small children in a two-room apartment really were rather intimidating. Nelli muttered something; she couldn't open her mouth properly without swallowing the pins she was using on the seam. Nelli held the half-finished dress together at Mari's back with one hand, took pins from the corner of her mouth with the other and stuck them into the material, quick as lightning. Up, down and up again, never sticking them into Mari's back.

Mari was getting restless. She had been standing still for so long that her arms and legs felt as if they were going to sleep. Mrs. Panacek was playing with Schurli on the other side of the bedroom door, which stood ajar. Perhaps she was doing something to him? Perhaps she was hugging him so tight he couldn't breathe? Or trying to pull one of his legs off? The things she was imagining almost made Mari break out in a sweat. Christi, the middle child, took the lid off the soup pot and looked in. Steam rose from it, and then Mari heard Nelli slapping Christi's fingers. "Oh, for goodness' sake!" exclaimed Nelli.

The twins were sitting in the corner of the kitchen, making faces at Mari and grinning. The radio was on; it was even noisier than Schurli. At last Mari was allowed to get out of the dress, very carefully, because of the pins.

While Nelli cleared toys off the table to make room for the half-finished dress, Mari went into the bedroom. Schurli had stopped crying. He was beaming at Mrs. Panacek, who was lying on her back like a beetle, legs in the air, waving them about.

"Da-da," said Schurli.

"I'm a cyclist on a hill climb," said Mrs. Panacek solemnly.

"Not on the floor!" said Mari, unsure whether or not to laugh. "The floor's so cold."

Mrs. Panacek was wearing nothing but a thin skirt, which had slipped up as far as her underwear, showing her two odd stockings. They were full-length knitted stockings, held in place with elastic garters above the knee.

"It's cold in the mountains too," she said. "There's snow up there."

And she went on waving her legs. Schurli liked it. Mari

laughed, and Nelli came in carrying Christi. She shook her head, amused.

"Hey, your friend's a bit crazy, isn't she?" she said to Mari, but her voice sounded kind.

Mari was relieved to find that Nelli didn't seem to mind Mrs. Panacek's behavior. Perhaps because Nelli herself was rather crazy, thought Mari. Or no, Nelli wasn't really crazy, she simply didn't mind what people said, and went ahead and acted the way she liked.

However, Mari felt she owed Nelli an explanation. "Mrs. Panacek lives at the Alder Yard Home."

"What, with all the loonies?" asked Nelli. She let Christi slide to the floor. "My mom was once in there too."

"Was she?" asked Mari. She couldn't imagine it. Mrs. Schumeier was caretaker of the community center in Wisgrill Street, and lived in the same apartment building as Hilde, Mari's best friend. Mari and Hilde often used to run away from Mrs. Schumeier. When she caught children putting their chewing gum under the banisters of the building or riding up and down in the elevator she would scream like a fishwife. Had she really been in Alder Yard?

"Had a rotten time there too," said Nelli, frowning.

Mrs. Panacek picked Schurli out of his cot and hugged him. "You mustn't put him behind bars," she told Nelli.

"Hm," said Nelli, shrugging her shoulders. "He'd be under my feet the whole time if I didn't! No, let her be," she said to Mari. "She won't hurt Schurli."

Suddenly Mari felt extraordinarily lighthearted: a sensation beginning somewhere deep within her and rising right up to her head. Nelli was marvelous! Good grief, think what a fuss Granny would have made if Mari had taken Mrs. Panacek home! And how about her parents? Mari wasn't too sure what her parents would do in a case like that. They'd be polite, she knew, but anxious too, and if Mrs.

Panacek suddenly began her cycling exercises they'd be even more worried. Mother might even sneak away and call the police.

"It'll be ready Tuesday."

Mari turned her head and looked at Nelli, confused. "What?"

"The dress," said Nelli. She laughed. "Why are you looking like that?"

"I'm okay," Mari assured her. Her face was hot. Mari flushed whenever she felt she'd been caught.

"By the beautiful Blue Danube," sang Mrs. Panacek, waltzing through the kitchen with Schurli. She snatched up a reel of cotton from the table and held it in front of Schurli's nose. The little boy beamed. The twins laughed. Nelli whistled "The Blue Danube." Christi's face crumpled up as if she were about to cry. Mari laughed, and the potatoes burned in their pan.

"Oh, no—they'll be ruined!" Nelli ran to the stove and snatched the pan off the burner. "What a mess!"

"Set the table," she told the twins, who trotted off obediently. Nelli wiped her hands on her stomach; they hurt from the hot pan.

It was time for Mari to go. "I'm off, then," she said. "*We're* off," she corrected herself.

"Right," said Nelli absently, looking for a sharp knife. "See you Tuesday, then?"

"See you Tuesday," said Mari. She took Schurli away from Mrs. Panacek and put him down on the floor. Schurli started to howl.

"Ba-ba," said Mrs. Panacek sadly. She went over to Nelli, put her hand on Nelli's pregnant bulge and stroked it. Then she let Mari take her hand and lead her away.

6

"WHATEVER kept you so long at Nelli's?"

Mother put a plate of soup with semolina dumplings in front of Mari. It was too full. A small wave of soup slopped over the edge, but the tablecloth soaked it up.

"Nothing much," said Mari, shrugging her shoulders. "I was trying the dress on."

"For two hours?"

"We played with Schurli," Mari said.

Mother sat down opposite Mari and watched her eat. "What's the matter with you?" Mother asked. "There's *something* the matter with you."

Mari did not reply. Mother sighed, and looked away from her daughter, staring into the middle distance as she thought out loud. "Trust and understanding, so important in a child's upbringing!" she said sadly. "And I've tried so hard. You've always been able to tell me anything, haven't you?"

Silence.

"I met Grete in the street today," said Mother. Mari raised an inquiring eyebrow, and an alarm bell went off in her head. Meeting Mother's friend Grete in the street meant hearing a whole load of gossip.

Mother's fingers were tapping nervously at the underside of the table. Mari listened uneasily to the sound. It was all right so long as the tapping went on, but if it stopped, that meant Mother had come upon a piece of old chewing gum. Mari always parked her chewing gum there to be reused, from motives of economy, even when there was no sweetness left in it at all. That was something Mother didn't understand.

"Mari, have you been meeting that old woman again?"

The tapping had stopped. Looking disgusted, Mother removed her hand from under the table.

"Sometimes," said Mari, counting the dumplings left in her soup. Two and a half.

"Father and I wish you wouldn't," said Mother.

"I know, I *know*," said Mari. Her spoon splashed back into the soup, and spots of grease were sprinkled over her skirt and sweater and the tablecloth. She jumped up and ran out of the kitchen.

"Mari!" called Mother. She had never seen Mari so angry before! Mother immediately started to wonder where she got it from; certainly not from *her!*

Outside the kitchen, Mari leaned against the door and tried to keep back her tears. She couldn't; how silly! And she didn't even know why she was crying.

"Hi!"

Tommy bumped into Mari. She had seen him from a long way off, and knew he wouldn't just let her pass. Tommy was tough. As he came closer, Mari tensed her stomach muscles, but she dared not cross to the other side of the street, although Tommy had never done anything bad to her, except bumping into her all the time. Well, he did once trip her during break at school.

So why, Mari wondered, am I scared of him? She was still wondering long after Tommy had disappeared down the underpass below the railway. Maybe it's the way he looks. Sort of fiendish. Really weird.

Mother was staying late at the office this afternoon; she had to take over for someone else who was sick. Granny had said she couldn't put off her appointment at the doctor's any longer. Thank goodness for that, thought Mari. And since Father was busy with his nineteenth-century film till evening, Mari had to amuse herself today.

Where could Mrs. Panacek be? Mari had not seen her on the bench near the church for two whole days. She had just been there. This was the third day.

The blind beggar with the dark glasses was sitting outside Schütz's Hairdressing Salon. Mari went the long way around to avoid him. Automatically, she walked on to the movie theater and looked at the stills outside, without really seeing them.

The matinee performance was just over, and Mari was almost swept away by the excited crowd coming out of the theater. Mainly children, only a few grown-ups. Not many grown-ups go to see children's films.

Mari wasn't allowed to go to the movies very often.

"What a super film," said a voice behind her. Mari jumped. "Golly, yes!" said a second, affected voice. Silly cows. Hilde and Veronica. Acting as if they hadn't seen Mari, although they couldn't have missed her.

And to think that only two weeks ago, at the school concert, Hilde had assured her, "You're my very best friend, Mari. You're not like that silly peroxide blonde!"

The silly peroxide blonde was Veronica, of the affected

voice. She was just too pretty to be true. She looked like a princess, which was why she got the part of the golden-haired heroine in the end-of-term play, the part that was to have been Mari's. Because Mrs. Brauer had fallen for Veronica's fair hair. And Mari could have borrowed a lovely blond wig from Aunt Anna.

Mari felt like grinding her teeth as her ex-best friend and the peroxide blonde disappeared from sight, arm in arm and giggling. She wasn't going to show it, but she was near tears. She didn't know what was the matter with her these days, any more than her parents did. She'd heard them discussing her yesterday, saying maybe she was depressed, you did get children suffering from depression these days. Father had muttered something about prepuberty, looking hard at Mari. Wondering if she was growing little breasts yet, because of the prepuberty. She wasn't, but that peroxide blonde was. Mari dug her hands angrily into her pockets and did a sharp about-face. Home again. Past the mustard and vinegar factory. There was a smell of mustard and vinegar.

Through the underpass. Twenty-six steps down, twenty-six steps up. Two exits in between, one for the West Station, one for St. Pölten.

Ahead of her, a boy was pushing a squeaky bike along. A man wearing baggy trousers was standing face to the wall with his legs apart; there was a splashing sound. Mari held her nose. The whole underpass smelled like a huge lavatory. The model girls on the posters had mustaches, and bits of poster had been torn away between their legs.

Mari always hurried through the underpass. It was not nice down there. They said a little girl had been found there dead a few years ago. The place gave her the creeps, and she did not breathe freely again until she was back in the open air. The sun came out as she was passing Friedmann's Garden Shop, going toward the café. There was a strong smell of goulash. Mari's mouth watered. She had felt too lazy to warm up the beef olives left for her at lunchtime.

I might buy myself some sausages and goulash sauce, thought Mari. Barry the dog came out of the café garden, wagging his tail. He was almost as tall as Mari, but Mari wasn't afraid of him, because Barry had such a trusting look in his eyes.

She put a cautious hand on his coat. Barry didn't seem pleased. Or rather, thought Mari, a bit annoyed, he didn't seem to notice. Perhaps he couldn't even feel her loving him through his thick coat.

She walked through the café garden, gravel crunching underfoot. There were a couple of drunk men sitting at the worn green wooden tables. Mari could just hear Granny saying: In broad daylight too! The very idea! Though Mari supposed that if you were going to get drunk you could do it just as well in broad daylight; it had nothing to do with the time of day. She went up the two steps to the café, followed by Barry. The room smelled of smoke and grease.

"Sausages and goulash sauce, please," said Mari, stationing herself between the peanut vending machine and the glass case of filled rolls. The café proprietor nodded, and she waited.

"Seven . . . eight . . ." She heard coins clinking on a table top behind her. "One . . . two. . . ."

Mari turned around.

"Mrs. Panacek!" cried Mari, delighted. "Mrs. Panacek!" Mari sat down on the wooden bench beside her. "Where have you been all this time, Mrs. Panacek?"

"Seven . . . eight. . . ." Not to be distracted, Mrs. Panacek went on counting.

"Your sausages," said the proprietor, putting the plate in front of Mari. The plump sausages were swimming in red sauce.

"One . . . two. . . ." Mrs. Panacek hasn't done her hair today, thought Mari. She smells a bit, too.

"Yes, you've got eight schillings there," said Mari impatiently, stretching her hand out toward the coins.

"No!" said Mrs. Panacek sharply. At last she looked at Mari. Angrily at first, but in a moment the lines on her forehead were smoothed away, and she smiled. "Yes, eight schillings." She smiled again, and stroked Mari's hair.

She hasn't cleaned her teeth either, thought Mari. It occurred to her that she hadn't cleaned her own teeth today.

"I'm so glad to see you," said Mari to Mrs. Panacek's smiling face. She dug her fork into one of the sausages, lifted it out of the goulash sauce and offered it to Mrs. Panacek, who didn't take it.

"I'll get fat," muttered Mari, munching the sausage.

"Eight schillings," repeated Mrs. Panacek.

Mari wished she would stop going on about it. Here was Mari, so pleased to have found Mrs. Panacek again, and instead of being pleased herself, Mrs. Panacek was just counting her silly money.

"The figure of eight lies on its back," remarked Mrs. Panacek.

"What?" said Mari, with her mouth full and a bit of sausage sticking out between the teeth she hadn't cleaned today. Puzzled, she stared at Mrs. Panacek.

"The number eight's important!" said Mrs. Panacek. "Karl was born on the eighth day of the eighth month in 1908," she told Mari proudly, raising her voice. It was too loud. The building workers at the next table were already laughing at the funny old woman.

"At eight o'clock, I bet," Mari guessed.

"Of course. Is it eight o'clock now?" Mrs. Panacek looked anxiously at the greasy, smoke-blackened clock above the doorway. Couldn't she tell the time?

"It's just after five," Mari told her. "Five past five," she added.

"Eight minutes to eight." Mrs. Panacek looked as if she were in dead earnest.

"No, five past five!" Mari repeated, her head to one side.

"Eight minutes to eight to eight eighteighteight . . ." Mrs. Panacek went on saying "eighteighteight" like a record stuck in a groove, and at each "eight" a coin came down on the table. Two of them fell off and rolled away on the floor. She did not laugh.

Mari pushed away her empty plate and disappeared under the table. She found first one of the coins and then the other in the dark there.

Mrs. Panacek's red stocking glowed in the dark. There was a tear in her long skirt, which was hitched up over one knee. That knee looked grazed and very dirty. She must have fallen over. When, and where?

Up above her, Mrs. Panacek was tracing figures of eight in the goulash sauce with her left forefinger. "Eight," she muttered, her voice rising and falling as she drew the figures of eight.

"The old bag's crazy!" said one of the building workers at the next table out loud. His friends roared with laughter and slapped their thighs.

Mrs. Panacek heard the men and looked at them. Looked at them hard. Suddenly they were very quiet.

"Old witch," muttered one of them, a red-haired man, glancing away.

Mari was furious. She imagined what she'd say to those men if—well, if she only dared! The fact that she did not dare made her even angrier.

"Here, tell her to behave herself." The waiter was leaning down to whisper in Mari's ear. She had not noticed him coming up to the table. "It's disgusting, dabbling about in the sauce like that," he said, raising his voice. "Enough to make my customers leave."

Mrs. Panacek took her finger out of the sauce and showed it to him. "Very good!" she praised the sauce.

He turned away in disgust, and then turned back, picked up the plate and told Mari curtly, "That'll be five schillings."

Mari paid. "Come along, Mrs. Panacek," she said. She and Mrs. Panacek made their way past Barry, whose tongue was lolling out, hanging down to the ground. Mari patted him again. The waiter stacked beer glasses noisily in the sink, with a last brief glance at the peculiar old woman and the little girl. He was glad to see the backs of them.

Out on the sidewalk, Mari put Mrs. Panacek's money into the purse the old woman wore around her neck. "Eight schillings, yes, my eight schillings!" said Mrs. Panacek gratefully, patting her money. "All I have in the world."

"I haven't got *any* money left," said Mari regretfully.

Mrs. Panacek began to run, faster and faster, too fast for Mari to keep up. "Wait for me, Mrs. Panacek!" she cried.

Mrs. Panacek did not hear, but she let the breathless Mari catch up to her. "Oh, Mrs. Panacek!" exclaimed Mari. Two little streams were running down the woman's cheeks, trickling into the neck of her sweater. "Mrs. Panacek!" said Mari, horrified. "Why are you crying? Tell me!"

Mrs. Panacek walked on in silence.

"Mrs. Panacek!"

Mrs. Panacek stopped, bowing her head. Mari did not know whether to walk on, expecting Mrs. Panacek to follow her, or stop too, or what? If only she would stop crying.

"I'm not going back," Mrs. Panacek suddenly sobbed.

"Going back where?" asked Mari, but she could guess what was coming next. She guessed that Mrs. Panacek had run away from the Home. You could tell from her torn skirt that she must have spent the night out of doors somewhere.

Mari looked at the time. Nearly five-thirty. Father came home at six, and Mother would be back at half past. So she couldn't go home now! And she couldn't leave Mrs. Panacek there in the middle of the street—not when she'd just found her, and when she was in such a state too.

Mari's mind worked feverishly. "Rotating the gray matter" Father used to call it when Mari stood thinking like that—fists clenched inside her pants pockets, lower lip thrust out. I have to be home at six, or just before, Mari thought. But I can't let Mrs. Panacek sleep outdoors.

"Did you sleep in the park, Mrs. Panacek?" she asked.

In point of fact, Mrs. Panacek had slept in the warm but dirty waiting room on a railway station platform, but Mari did not know that, and as Mrs. Panacek thought sleeping in the park didn't sound like a bad idea, she agreed. "Yes, I slept in the park." She went on crying.

Mari decided to take Mrs. Panacek home with her after all. To her own room. Father wouldn't come in there after eight, and if she made sure Mrs. Panacek left their apartment and went back to the Alder Yard Home before six in the morning, no one would ever know.

Mrs. Panacek had calmed down. She sniffed, and stared at Mari's nose.

Why had she run away from the Home? Mari decided to clear that one up later; there wasn't time now. She had to make up her mind.

"Would you like to come home with me, Mrs. Panacek?" asked Mari. Mrs. Panacek was still staring at her nose. "Have I got a fly on it, or what?" Mari rubbed her nose nervously.

"No, just a little red spot," said Mrs. Panacek solemnly, putting out her hand as if to squeeze the spot for Mari.

"Not now," said Mari impatiently.

"Now is the time for everything," said Mrs. Panacek.

"Not for squeezing spots," said Mari. Mrs. Panacek sometimes seemed like a very small child. Although, in a way, what she said about now being the time for everything . . . well, that was really how things should be, wasn't it?

Oh, never mind, thought Mari. I want a sensible answer out of her for once. She *can* be sensible if she likes. "Would you like to come home with me or not?"

"Eight schillings," said Mrs. Panacek, tapping her purse with a wealth of meaning. "Eight schillings. I shall go to a hotel!"

Well, at least she understands what I'm talking about, thought Mari. "Oh, Mrs. Panacek, you do make things difficult for me." She sighed.

"That's what they all say," Mrs. Panacek agreed sadly.

Mari was alarmed. "I didn't mean it that way," she said gently.

"Don't be sad," Mrs. Panacek told her. "You must laugh!"

"Who, me? When? Now? No, no!" said Mari, taking Mrs. Panacek's hand and pulling her along. "Look, we don't have time now—not for anything."

And Mari talked on and on, not allowing herself to be interrupted by Mrs. Panacek telling her that people ought to laugh. "Listen, we have to be home before six because that's when Father comes in. And he mustn't see you, Mrs. Panacek because, you see—well, he'd make you leave, and then you'd have to sleep under the bridge or in the park, and probably graze your other knee, and . . ."

People turned and stared in surprise at the strange couple hurrying along Cumberland Street. It looked almost as if the little girl in the black slacks and yellow sweater were kidnapping the untidy old woman in the torn skirt.

And really, thought Mari, not caring a bit about the staring people, really that wasn't so far away from the truth.

7

MARI was assailed by doubts on the stairs. She had broken out into a sweat down below, when they passed Dr. Wiesner the pediatrician's door. Suppose the door opened, which would not be at all surprising at this time of day, and Dr. Wiesner or his daughter Lieselotte saw Mrs. Panacek? The Home was sure to have reported her missing to the police. In fact, Mari was rather surprised that no policeman had bothered to look out for a lost or runaway mental patient in the street.

But they reached the second floor without being seen.

"Wait a moment," said Mari. She lifted the doormat, and there was the silvery gleam of a key underneath.

Mrs. Panacek was sweating and panting.

They could hear the voice of the woman next door from her kitchen window, which looked out on the corridor. Mari quickly unlocked the front door, and heaved a sigh of relief. The apartment was empty—for the moment. The hands of the old clock in the hall said ten to six.

"Into my room," Mari told Mrs. Panacek, and the fugitive obediently trotted after her.

In fact, there was order in the chaos of Mari's room, but the main thing was that Mari could find her own way around it. Mrs. Panacek seemed to like it. She sat straight down on the floor, saying, "Nice!" and stroked the carpet.

"No, no, you must climb up there, Mrs. Panacek!"

"Up there?" Mrs. Panacek looked anxiously at the wobbly ladder up to the top bunk of the bunk beds by the wall opposite the window. The bunk beds had been put together by Mother herself as Mari's birthday present, because Mari wanted Hilde to be able to come and stay the night any time. Hilde . . . huh!

Mari was already pushing and heaving Mrs. Panacek up the ladder to the top bunk. Just for this one night . . .

Mari climbed up after her. "Lie down, please, Mrs. Panacek," she whispered, piling pillows and blankets on top of the old woman. "You're not frightened, are you?" she asked. But it was her own voice that trembled, not Mrs. Panacek's when she said, "No, I'm not frightened today."

Mari stared. "You mean you *often* get frightened?"

"Yes," said Mrs. Panacek, looking so sad it almost made Mari cry. "Yes, I often get frightened. I've been frightened all my life."

Mari stood there on the ladder, not sure what to do next. Up or down? Father would be home any moment.

"Mari?"

Mari was already down the ladder when Mrs. Panacek peered over the side of the bunk bed, evidently wanting something.

"I need the bathroom."

"Oh, *no!*" wailed Mari. She dashed to the front door, put the chain across it, and was showing Mrs. Panacek the way to the bathroom as Father put his key in the lock from the other side and found he couldn't get in.

[50]

"Mari! Mari!" he shouted impatiently. The door creaked and rattled; Father was shaking it.

"Coming!" Mari shouted back. "I'm in the bathroom! *Quick!*" she whispered, flushing the toilet for Mrs. Panacek, who had forgotten to do it because she had to pull her underwear up so fast. Mari shooed Mrs. Panacek back up the ladder to the top bunk again.

"And please keep quiet!" she begged. Mrs. Panacek anxiously nodded her head, and disappeared under the mound of pillows. "Here!" said Mari, chucking up a handful of Mickey Mouse comics.

"*Mari!*" shouted Father, sounding very angry by now. Mari raced through the hall and almost fell flat on her face. "You're as red as a lobster," said Father. "Have you got a temperature, or have we all gone crazy, or what?"

"Oh, no, nothing like that. I've been in the bathroom. I have diarrhea."

"Oh?" Father looked at Mari suspiciously.

"Yes, honestly." Mari nodded, hoping Father had wax in his ears, because otherwise he'd be sure to hear how loud her heart was beating. He went into the kitchen and looked around it, disappointed.

"Nothing to eat? Where's Mother?" He had forgotten that Mother was working late today. He gave himself a shake—you could actually see him doing it—and said, "I'll cook something then."

Father did not like cooking, and he was not very good at it. Mari stood in the kitchen doorway, her cheeks burning, keeping one ear on her own room as she watched Father prepare the meal. He opened a can of sausages, chopped some onions, skinned the sausages, and said reproachfully, "Aren't you going to help me?"

"I don't feel well," said Mari.

Father did not reply.

"I feel sick."

"You'll soon be better," said Father absently, right hand feeling for the switch of the radio.

"I think I'll go to bed," said Mari, just as the radio blared out.

"What?" Father shouted above the music.

"Nothing," Mari replied quickly, because it had just occurred to her that if she did go to bed her parents might come to her room to see how she was. "I'm going to the bathroom again."

"Right," said Father, blowing at the gas flame on the stove.

Mari went to the bathroom and locked herself in.

What had she let herself in for this time?

She stayed sitting in the bathroom for almost ten minutes, listening to the various different noises in the building. Someone was flushing another toilet either above or below her. A radio was playing. She heard wood creaking, and something going plop somewhere. A drop of water splashed into the blue hand-basin. Fat sizzled in the pan in the kitchen.

She put her ear to the wall on the right. Her own room lay beyond it. And Mrs. Panacek would be lying there on the other side of the wall at about the height of the medicine cabinet. Her feet would be there, and her head over there. Her crazy mixed-up head.

No crazier than mine, I bet, thought Mari. At this rate I'll soon go crazy. They mustn't find her. But even if they *don't* find her I'll go crazy worrying that they *will* find her.

And if they *do* find Mrs. Panacek, they'll think I *am* crazy, asking a crazy person to my room, and one way and another I will go crazy.

Mari put paper down the toilet and flushed it. The toilet paper danced down into the dark pipe in a little whirlpool of water.

How she ever got through the next hour and a half in the kitchen Mari could not have said later. All she remembered was the taste of the potato goulash (because however hard you brush your teeth, the flavor of onions hangs around), and the worried expression on Mother's face. She also re-membered pushing Mother's hand away when Mother laid it on her forehead to see if she had a temperature. But all Mother said was, "Now, now!" She wasn't angry; she was only very, very worried.

Father was in a good mood; he had had a successful day, and then made a good potato goulash, which everyone en-joyed. He knew Mari was always inclined to toy with her food, so he didn't take that as an insult to his culinary talents.

Mari must have eaten her supper without even noticing. She kept imagining Mrs. Panacek up on the top bunk of the bed, with her face mirroring her thoughts: Shall I climb down and look for Mari or shall I stay here like she told me?

"Good night," Mari said perfunctorily to Mother. She kissed both her parents and disappeared into her bedroom.

"Prepuberty," Father muttered.

"Who knows?" said Mother, and later, when Mari had been in her room some time, Mother tried to open the door. She couldn't, because Mari had locked it. She knocked at the door and called out, with forced gaiety, "Pining for love of someone, Mari?"

Mari held her breath as Mother tried to open the door, and heaved a sigh of relief when things were quiet again.

"She's gone," she told Mrs. Panacek, who had clasped her hands behind her head and was lying on her back, eyes half closed.

"Do you like it here?" Mari plucked at Mrs. Panacek's sleeve.

Instead of replying, Mrs. Panacek flickered her eyelashes,

and Mari realized for the first time that you can talk without using words.

She put her head on one side, and studied Mrs. Panacek, lying there so peacefully. "You can only stay till tomorrow morning, though, Mrs. Panacek," she said in a low voice, so that no ear laid against the door could hear her.

"He won't come here," said Mrs. Panacek, turning her head and looking at Mari, eyes very wide. "He won't come here."

"No, of course not," said Mari. "Father wouldn't let him in. He never lets strangers in unless he knows them." Mari thought for a moment. "But then, of course, they wouldn't be strangers."

"Once upon a time," said Mrs. Panacek out of the blue, "I was a very beautiful young woman."

Mari put two pillows underneath her and settled herself comfortably, sitting cross-legged. She was glad Mrs. Panacek had started talking and didn't look frightened or sad. It sounded as if she were about to tell Mari her life history.

She sounds like a perfectly normal person now, thought Mari.

"Yes, I was very beautiful, my father always said so. He said he loved me best of all the five of us."

"Five? Were there really five children in your family?" asked Mari.

"Yes, there was Elizabeth, Gisela, Angelica and Editha. All girls. And Maria."

"That's you." Mari nodded.

"That's me. I'm the only one left. The others have all gone away." Mrs. Panacek was looking sad again. There was a small, melancholy pause. "Two of them got married and went to live in Czechoslovakia, and now they can't get out again. Or perhaps they don't want to anymore. Angi and her husband emigrated to America, and I haven't heard from Gisela since—since . . ."

She said no more for a long, long time. Mari didn't know if it was only a pause or the end of the story.

"We grew up in the cemetery." Mrs. Panacek laid a finger on her lips.

"The cemetery?" Mari shivered.

"Our father was the caretaker and head gardener there, and Mother had a stall opposite the cemetery gates. She sold flowers and candles. We were very respectable, oh, yes! People looked up to us. And I was the apple of my father's eye. Because I was the youngest, you see. No boys were even allowed to look at me—it made my father furious. Oh, he got really jealous if a boy stared at me on Sunday after church. He'd take me home right away. 'Maria's not for the likes of him,' he'd say. It was different with Gisela, she was ugly, he said. 'Let *her* go around with men,' he said, 'we should be glad anybody wants her!' I had to go to homemaking school. Oh, my father was very strict."

Another pause. Mari listened. The television was on full blast next door.

Mrs. Panacek must be seeing everything just the way it used to be in her mind's eye, thought Mari. Herself when she was young and beautiful, her sisters and her father and mother. I wonder what they looked like. I wonder if she has any photographs of them. Maybe at the Home?

"I was thirty before I met Karl. Ah, Karl . . ." Mrs. Panacek sighed deeply. "He had a fishmonger's shop. He was so handsome—a fine figure of a man. So tall and strong! When I first saw him, I was out shopping with Mother and I knew he was the man for me. I can still see him"—she laughed quietly—"with a carp in his hand, holding it up in the air. The creature was still alive. And then he looked into my eyes, still holding that carp up in the air. There was blood on his apron; you get that in a fishmonger's. It was very romantic. I stood there beside my mother, drowning in Karl's eyes, and he was drowning in mine, and Mother said something sharp, and the fish slipped out of his hand and fell on the stone floor. I laughed so loud that my mother laughed too at first, and then she slapped me because she thought I was having hysterics. I cried, and Karl went crawling about the floor after the carp. . . ."

Mari laughed, and so did Mrs. Panacek. Mrs. Panacek giggled, and so did Mari. She could just imagine it: the tall fishmonger trying to retrieve his carp, and Mrs. Panacek, the lovely Maria, standing in his shop in a long white dress, and her mother slapping her face so that her mascara ran. . . . "Did they have mascara in those days?" asked Mari.

"Goodness, no!" Mrs. Panacek looked at Mari in amazement. "Oh, no, you weren't allowed to use makeup; you'd have got a shocking reputation! Karl put his carp back in the water, and he took off his apron while Mother was paying the old lady. He came running after me and Mother; he wanted to find out where I lived! Mother thought that was very forward of him, and she walked faster and faster, tugging me along by the hand."

"And in the end you married the fishmonger, Mrs. Panacek?"

"Yes," said Mrs. Panacek. "Yes, I married Karl Panacek. It was the love of our lives, for both of us. Karl was my great love and I was his. Of course, we wanted to get married at once, but Father wouldn't agree for two years, not until the old lady was dead. Because the shop didn't belong to Karl until she died, and Father wanted security for me. Yes, indeed. . . ."

Mrs. Panacek's mind was straying into the past. Mari would have loved to be able to see all that Mrs. Panacek was seeing now. Why can't you give your memories away? Or at least lend them, just for a few minutes?

"Karl was so pleased about the children," Mrs. Panacek whispered. "Quite wild with joy, he was! And they were all the very image of him, as if I'd had nothing to do with it. We were married for fifteen years, three months and four days."

"And then did you get divorced?" asked Mari, curiously.

"He fell down dead. Just as if he'd been struck by lightning. One minute he was alive, the next he was dead. It was in the shop."

"He simply fell down dead?" Mari felt a shiver running down her spine.

"Mm." Mrs. Panacek nodded. "Then he was gone. The Lord gave and the Lord has taken away. I went on running the shop. Oh, I was very good at the business! I don't mean that Karl wasn't good at the business too, but I had a real feel for the fish trade. The children were still at school, but they had to help out in the afternoons. A real family business, we were. Only I couldn't live in the apartment anymore. . . ." Mrs. Panacek's voice dropped, and she sat up, grunting a little. She huddled into a ball. "I moved into a new one with the children. We could afford it. But all the same, I kept on the old apartment where Karl and I used to live. I couldn't have stood seeing strangers move in. I didn't want anything altered. I went to the old apartment every day after the shop closed and lit a couple of candles for Karl. The children didn't know. And I went there on weekends too. Then I started going there more and more, and Karin, my eldest, she looked after the shop. I only went into the shop once a week. You understand, don't you?"

Mari jumped in alarm as two hands came out to seize her. Mrs. Panacek was shaking her.

"You understand, don't you? I'd slaved long enough! I was entitled to take it easy, wasn't I?"

"Yes," said Mari, scared.

Mrs. Panacek dropped her hands to her lap. "I couldn't stand the sight of fish anymore," she confessed. "But all the same"—she sat up and tried to smooth out her creased skirt—"all the same, it was still *my* shop! He had no right to take it away from me."

"Your son-in-law?"

"The scoundrel! First seducing my daughter, then grabbing everything, and the State lets him, too!"

"The State?" Baffled, Mari looked at the excited red face opposite her.

"The State, yes! They took it away from me; they said I wasn't fit to run my own affairs, as if I was a baby! Just because the apartment burned down—"

"Which apartment?" asked Mari anxiously.

"Karl's and mine. I can do what I like with my own apartment! I can burn it down if I like!"

"But other apartments might burn down too," said Mari, her voice louder than she had intended. Thank goodness her parents were watching a football match on television next door.

"The other apartments weren't Karl's and mine," said Mrs. Panacek.

"No, that's what I mean," said Mari.

"I didn't let Karl burn," said Mrs. Panacek, looking at her hands as if she had suddenly grown a new pair.

"But you can't go burning apartments down."

"I could," said Mrs. Panacek. "It was my own property."

"No, you couldn't," said Mari.

Mrs. Panacek began to tremble, and then to cry. Mari put an arm around one of her legs in alarm. "It's all right," she said soothingly.

"They don't leave you anything," mumbled Mrs. Panacek. "Nothing. They take it all away. He wants to take my life away too."

"Who?"

"*Him.* The poisoner. He's got everything. He's got my

apartment, he's got my shop, he's got my daughter. And the day before yesterday he came to see me."

"At the Home, you mean? Alder Yard?"

"Yes, yes. He said it was because it was my birthday, but I don't have a birthday. It's a long, long time since I had a birthday. He gave me a package. He brought the child with him to make it look innocent. He said my daughter couldn't come because she had to stay in the shop. I dare say he'd been beating her again; she can't fight back. Oh, I kept quite calm until he'd gone. Very friendly, I was, so he wouldn't suspect. So he wouldn't realize I knew his plan!" Mrs. Panacek's eyes were very wide now. "When he'd gone I threw the package away. Over a fence. Maybe there was a cake in it—a poisoned cake. But suppose he realizes I'm not dead?" Mrs. Panacek's frightened eyes looked straight into Mari's. "Then he'll come back to the Home and make sure he kills me this time!"

"No, I'm sure he won't." Mari was shivering, and her teeth were chattering slightly. Was that because of the cold, or because she was getting as worked up as Mrs. Panacek?

"They never leave me in peace, not anywhere. I live in Alder Yard now. The people there are sometimes cross, but I have my bed there, and my things. Things from the old days, and my pictures and my doll. He wants *them* too."

Two large tears ran down Mrs. Panacek's cheeks. At first Mari didn't quite dare, but then she couldn't help herself: she hugged Mrs. Panacek hard and stroked her tangled gray hair. It smelled a little rancid, as if there were butter on it.

"Everything will be all right," said Mari, although she was not so sure of that herself. "Everything will be all right."

Her alarm clock said eleven-thirty. Only half an hour till midnight. "We must go to sleep," said Mari, quite alarmed. "Can you get to sleep, Mrs. Panacek?"

Mrs. Panacek nodded, and blew her nose on her skirt.

[59]

"Aren't you going to undress?"

Mrs. Panacek shook her head, and Mari climbed down the ladder and got into bed, still with her own clothes on, as a precaution, because who knew what else might happen tonight?

She set the alarm clock for half past five in the morning, made sure it would ring all right, and put all unpleasant thoughts out of her mind. She wasn't going to think of anything; she'd go straight off to sleep. And everything would be all right. She was sure it would.

8

MARI woke with a start, her heart beating very loud. She shook back her hair before groping for the alarm clock and switching it off at last.

A hand was dangling from the top bunk, above her.

Although Mari was usually still half asleep first thing in the morning, and had trouble remembering the events of the previous day, she realized at once that the hand must be Mrs. Panacek's.

The fingers of the hand moved.

"Mrs. Panacek?" said Mari softly.

By way of answer, there was a little cough and a little sigh, and the bed creaked.

Mari ran her fingers through her hair and went over to open the window. The room was stuffy. And no sooner was the window open than the feeling of fear was there in the room again, as if it had been lying patiently in wait outside the window all night.

[61]

There was gooseflesh on Mari's arms. She climbed up to the top bunk. "Time to get up, Mrs. Panacek," she said cautiously, plucking at Mrs. Panacek's elbow.

Mrs. Panacek suddenly sat up and stared at Mari. "I'm awake," she said. There was an anxious expression on her face, which was creased with sleep. "Must I go now?"

"Yes," said Mari simply. "Yes, please."

Mrs. Panacek set about the task of climbing down the ladder. First her foot groped for the top rung, feeling about until it was firmly in position; then she climbed down. The ladder creaked. Mari noticed a nail sticking out of one side. She held the ladder against the bunk beds so that Mrs. Panacek wouldn't fall.

Once down, Mrs. Panacek smoothed out her skirt, which looked even worse today.

"I need the bathroom again," said Mrs. Panacek, sounding ashamed, as if needing the toilet were something very bad. She was probably remembering how quickly she'd had to pop out of the bathroom again yesterday, with Father already knocking impatiently at the front door.

"Quietly, though!" begged Mari. "And don't flush it."

Mrs. Panacek nodded. Mari tiptoed ahead of her to the bathroom, her heart in her mouth. She just hoped all these alarms and excursions would be over *some*time.

Mrs. Panacek flushed the toilet after all. Mari's chin jutted, and she gritted her teeth. "Come out!" she hissed through the bathroom door.

Then the door of her parents' bedroom opened, with a squeal, and out came Mother, eyes swollen up the same as every morning, and groping about for her bathrobe belt the same as usual too.

"What's going on?" she asked, half asleep, peering through her slitlike eyes.

However, when the toilet was flushed a second time, and

Mother realized that while her daughter was standing *outside* the bathroom door, it was being flushed on the *inside*, she opened her eyes very wide indeed.

"Mari!" cried Mother, horrified. "Mari!"

And she flung the bathroom door open. There was Mrs. Panacek, just pulling her skirt down, with a pile of toilet paper lying coiled at her feet, because the holder had gone wrong ages ago, and as soon as you took one piece half the roll followed it.

Mother stood looking at Mrs. Panacek. Her jaw dropped. She was unable to say anything at all.

"This is Mrs. Panacek," said Mari, with an awkward gesture; it isn't easy introducing someone who is in the bathroom.

"Oh. Hello, Mrs. Panacek," said Mother slowly. She was still feeling the aftereffects of the shock. Her bathrobe fell open. She had nothing on underneath, and she began fishing for the belt again when she felt Mrs. Panacek's eyes resting on her navel. Meanwhile Mari had taken two cautious steps sideways, in preparation for flight.

Then Mother did something which surprised Mari. She closed the bathroom door from the outside, walked past Mari like a sleepwalker, went into the kitchen, went over to the fridge and then—what a mercy Granny wasn't here to see!—then, at a quarter to six in the morning, she took a bottle of beer out of the salad cooler where Father liked to keep beer, because he said it came out just the right temperature then.

"Have a glass," said Mari tremulously, nearly dropping the beer mug.

"Thank you."

The beer frothed up into a big head which spilled over and dripped on the floor.

"Hell," muttered Mother inelegantly. She dabbled her

bare toes in the puddle of beer as she took a long gulp. When Mrs. Panacek, still in the bathroom, flushed the toilet for the third time, Mother closed her eyes.

However, the woman she saw standing in the kitchen doorway after she had had two more gulps of beer was not a dream. She looked, thought Mari, like any perfectly ordinary madwoman who hasn't had enough sleep.

"Do sit down," Mother said tonelessly.

"Thank you," said Mrs. Panacek, and she did sit down.

Mother put her beer glass down in rather a hurry and closed the kitchen door. "My husband," she said, by way of explanation. She didn't want Father waking up yet; she wanted to deal with the situation on her own.

"What on earth was the idea, Marianne?" asked Mother sternly. She fished for her belt again; the thing had a mind of its own.

"If I hadn't brought her here she'd have had to sleep under the bridge," said Mari defiantly, looking at her toes, which made Mother say, "Look at me when I'm talking to you!"

Mari stared fixedly at Mother's nose.

"Nobody has to sleep under bridges," said Mother.

Mrs. Panacek looked from Mari to Mother and from Mother to Mari. "The spitting image of you!" she said.

"You think so?" said Mother, allowing this to distract her.

"Oh, yes," said Mrs. Panacek. "Now my children, they all look the image of Karl. People used to say he must have done it all himself without any help from me."

"Yes, fine," Mother interrupted. She didn't mean anything much by "Yes, fine," it was probably all she could think of to stem the flow of Mrs. Panacek's remarks. "Yes, fine," she said. "Are you the lady from—from the . . ." Mother could not quite bring out the words *mental hospital*. "From Alder Yard?"

Mari intercepted a helpless look from Mrs. Panacek. "Yes, she is," Mari answered for her.

"Hasn't she got a bed there?" said Mother, turning to Mari.

"Yes, but because of her son-in-law, the murderer, poisoning her. . . ."

Mother took another sip of beer, swallowed it the wrong way, and coughed. "Nonsense," she said.

"It's not nonsense," said Mari.

"It isn't?" said Mother, rather uncertainly.

"No," said Mari.

She told Mother all she knew, while Mrs. Panacek sat there licking her lips because she was thirsty too, until Mari found a glass in the cupboard and poured her a beer as well without interrupting her story.

"So that's how it is?" said Mother at the end, helplessly.

"Mm." Mari nodded.

"Something must be done," said Mother.

"Not the police!" cried Mrs. Panacek in alarm, because the thought of the police had just occurred to her: the police who came to fetch her when she was committed to the mental hospital and took her to Alder Yard by force, when all she wanted was to be left alone in her own apartment and burn everything that reminded her of Karl.

"No, no!" said Mother, who was not too fond of the police either, not since she'd been in a demonstration against the Vietnam war years and years ago and the police used tear gas to disperse the crowd. Her eyes had stung horribly for hours.

The sun was rising outside the kitchen window. "Look!" said Mrs. Panacek, arm outstretched, pointing to the window. "The sun!"

"Lovely, isn't it?" said Mari, glad of a change of subject.

"Same as every day." Mother morosely lit herself a cigarette.

"Oh, you never know," said Mrs. Panacek, with a mysterious wink.

"Yes, it might be gone tomorrow. Gone for ever. Fallen into the sea," said Mari, communicating with Mrs. Panacek by means of a swift glance.

"Oh, nonsense," said Mother, getting cross again and puffing smoke rings into the air. Then she jumped up.

Oh, mercy . . . Father! A pair of check slippers came shuffling through the hall.

"Mmph?" There he stood in the kitchen doorway, rubbing his sleepy eyes as he took in the occupants of the room.

"Good morning," he said to Mrs. Panacek, but he did not move toward her, nor did it look as if he were going to shake hands. He just stood rooted to the spot.

"This is Mrs. Panacek, the lady from Alder Yard," explained Mother, turning her back on Father and leaving him to it. Let *him* try sorting the situation out!

Mrs. Panacek gave Father a friendly smile.

"It's only six o'clock," he told Mari, rather sternly.

"Early to bed, early to rise, makes a man healthy, wealthy and wise," replied Mari, unable to think of anything else helpful. One might as well try to give moments like this the look of normality at least.

"Hardly the usual time for social calls, is it?" said Father, not one hundred percent pleasantly, through the rings of smoke curling up from Mother's cigarette. "Oh, for God's sake, must you smoke before breakfast?" he added. "You'll ruin your health."

"Huh!" muttered Mother. "You're a fine one to talk."

"Well," said Father, scratching his thigh just behind the first red stripe on his red-and-blue-striped bathrobe, "well, I'd better get shaved."

"I haven't shaved yet either," said Mari. Father cast her a hopeless sort of glance, and Mother put the kettle on for coffee.

[66]

"Will you stay for breakfast, Mrs. Panacek?" asked Mother, in such a friendly voice that Mari nearly fell off her chair.

Capricious, that was the word for Mother.

"Yes, I'm sure she will," said Mari, answering for Mrs. Panacek, who was gazing out of the window at the sun.

"Go downstairs and get some rolls out of the freezer," Mother told her.

For a moment Mari wondered whether it would be all right to leave Mrs. Panacek alone in the kitchen with Mother. The freezer was down in the basement of the building. Mari decided to risk it, and fished her shoes out from under the table. Mother couldn't actually bite Mrs. Panacek.

"How many?"

Mother counted on her fingers. Eight. Two each.

Mari went down.

When she came back again, her parents were sitting peacefully at the breakfast table with Mrs. Panacek, drinking coffee. "At last!" muttered Father, his mouth full of biscuit. "Shove them in the oven." He was so hungry that he hadn't been able to wait.

When the rolls were ready, Mari bit into the crisp golden crust of hers. Under Father's reproachful eye, Mother spread butter very thickly on the bottom half of her roll. Father was afraid Mother might get fat, although she was not at all inclined to put on weight. She was the skinny sort; she could eat what she liked and never get fat.

"Two inches," remarked Mari, munching, and looking thoughtfully at Father's stomach. She poked him with her forefinger beside the pajama button in the region of his navel.

"Are you crazy?" yelped Father, frowning, and Mrs. Panacek laughed. If Father *could* have got any redder he would have done so now.

He cleared his throat. Once, twice, three times. Then he

turned to Mrs. Panacek. "Have you," he asked, "been in this—er—Home a long time?"

"Yes," said Mrs. Panacek with a sad smile. "I went there when my second granddaughter was born."

"That's three years ago," said Mari. After last night she knew as much about the Panacek family as her own.

"And now you don't like it there anymore?" Father went on.

Not like it! What was Mrs. Panacek supposed to say to *that?* She could only begin telling her life story all over again, and while Mari might find the patience to listen, she couldn't count on Father. Nor Mother, though she wasn't thrown off balance as easily as Father. Mrs. Panacek put her legs neatly together, her head hunched down between her shoulders. She dropped a piece of roll and cherry jam, and Mother kindly bent to pick it up.

"Have you ever been there?" asked Mrs. Panacek, her voice very intense. "Have you ever been there?" she repeated. Louder this time. The coffee cup in her hand began to tremble in an alarming way—or no, it was her hand, not the cup trembling.

"No, I never have," said Father, pushing his plate to the middle of the table as a precautionary measure. Mari could see he was scared. Mother looked anxious, too, as she carefully put the piece of roll down in the ashtray, along with her two before-breakfast cigarette butts.

Mrs. Panacek leaned toward Mari, who was on her left. She was getting worked up. "Does he know him?"

"Know who?"

"The murderer!"

"What murderer?" exclaimed Father, going pale around the nose.

"She means her son-in-law," Mari told her parents. "No, how could he know him?" she said to Mrs. Panacek.

[68]

"You're sure?" Mrs. Panacek asked suspiciously.

"I'm sure," said Mari, and a few of the thousand wrinkles in the old woman's face smoothed out.

"Will somebody kindly explain what's going on here, or am I to be left in the dark?"

Left in the dark, Mari would have liked to say, but instead she told her father, a note of pleading in her voice, "I'll tell you about it later."

"She'll tell you about it later." Mother echoed her words. "It would take too long now."

Father looked at the time, got up and said, "I'd better go."

In fact, it was too early for him to be leaving; he usually went out at seven-thirty. But Mari didn't mention that. She could well imagine that Father would be thankful to be out of the place and among the supposedly normal again.

Helplessly, almost pleadingly, Mother looked at him. "Don't go," she said. "Why do I have to take care of Mari all on my own? She's your daughter too!"

Father shrugged his shoulders uncertainly, and went out. There was silence in the kitchen.

"Er—do you take pills?" Mother asked nervously at last. "Regularly?"

"Yes," said Mrs. Panacek.

"And if you don't take them—I mean, do you have some with you?"

"Only two. I go easy with them. They're in my pocket."

Mother's expression became panic-stricken. She obviously expected Mrs. Panacek to start raving any minute now. "What happens if you don't take your pills?" Mother asked, her voice trembling.

"I get frightened," said Mrs. Panacek.

"I see," said Mother, sounding relieved that that was all that happened.

"Oh, then you must take your pills!" said Mari.

"No, no," cried Mrs. Panacek, drumming her fingers on her knees. "They don't help when I'm frightened of *that!*"

"Frightened of what?"

"Frightened of what that murderer Leopold may do!"

"You *must* go back to the Home," said Mother firmly. "I mean, that's where you live."

Mrs. Panacek looked out of the window again.

"Where else would you go?" Mother took Mrs. Panacek by the shoulders; even without shoes on, Mother was a good bit taller than Mrs. Panacek.

"No!" said Mrs. Panacek, terrified, looking at Mother's hands.

Mother's conscience smote her. She let go and looked at her own hands in surprise.

Mari was feeling unhappy. Mother didn't understand. Perhaps she didn't *want* to understand how frightened Mrs. Panacek was of Leopold, the murderer. She didn't know enough about Mrs. Panacek. Murderer—well, Leopold wasn't really a murderer; Mari knew Mrs. Panacek was only imagining things. And what had she expected? Had she really thought her parents would welcome Mrs. Panacek with open arms, saying: How nice to have you here. Yes, of course there's room in our little apartment for a madwoman on the run, do stay!

While Mrs. Panacek studied the calendar on the wall, her eyes wandering over the photograph at the head of the columns of dates, Mari stood on tiptoe and whispered in her mother's ear, "I'll take her back, Mother."

Mother sighed with relief, and stroked her daughter's hair. "Too much social conscience, that's your trouble," she said with a touch of pride. She and Mari hurriedly cleared away the breakfast things.

Mrs. Panacek watched the table getting emptier and

emptier, until there was nothing left but the shabby old wooden surface Mari was so fond of because you could scratch anything you liked on it. Even hearts saying MOTHER LOVES FATHER, or things like GRANNY IS CRAZY, although she had crossed that one out with her ballpoint pen until you couldn't tell what it said, the moment she had written it.

Mari's school was on Fichtner Street. It took her twenty minutes to get there if she went by bus, but she usually walked. When she was still at primary school, she'd been able to leave home at two minutes to eight and still be in her classroom on the dot of eight.

"Got your schoolbag ready?" Mother asked her, the same as she did every morning before she went into the bathroom. Irresolutely, Mrs. Panacek stood up. All this coming and going flustered her.

"Come with me," Mari told her in a whisper. "We're going!" she called to Mother through the bathroom door. The door opened, Mother took her toothbrush out of her mouth, said, "Good-bye," to Mrs. Panacek, gave Mari another meaningful look and went on brushing. Toothpaste foam splashed to the floor.

Mari walked so fast that Mrs. Panacek could hardly keep up with her. "Listen, I can't skip school," she was explaining. "You do see, Mrs. Panacek, don't you? But I'll be out at twelve today, because there's no gym lesson."

She glanced at the sky; it was going to be a fine day. Cold but sunny.

"Here, I'll give you twenty schillings." She pressed a twenty-schilling note, her emergency reserve fund, into the breathless Mrs. Panacek's hand as they walked on. "Go to the café in Nissel Street. And don't do anything silly. I promise I'll come and find you there at twelve, okay?"

She stopped at last, remorseful, realizing Mrs. Panacek couldn't keep going any longer. She had simply stopped in the middle of Diesterweg Street, exhausted. Luckily it was on the crosswalk. Yes, said Mrs. Panacek, she knew the Nissel Street café. She promised to wait there. But she looked so sad and forlorn that Mari very nearly decided to skip school after all, so as not to leave her on her own.

"Nothing can happen to you, honestly it can't!" she assured Mrs. Panacek, and then raced off, turned to wave, nearly stumbled over an extra-long dachshund with extra-long ears, and, breathless from running, just managed to catch the last bus that could get her to school on time.

9

HILDE was still ignoring her today. As soon as the bell rang she ran off to meet peroxide-blond Veronica, and the pair of them disappeared into Mrs. Glaser's sweet shop. Mari badly wanted to buy a sausage roll, but she wouldn't have gone into Mrs. Glaser's for the world. I'd rather starve to death, she swore, clenching her fists. No one ought to go around with people like that, not unless they have to.

In any case, she had something more pressing to do. Mrs. Panacek was waiting for her in the Nissel Street café, or so she hoped.

The bus smelled of leather schoolbags and the sweaty gym things some disgusting people kept on under their other clothes. As usual, Mari felt annoyed when none of the grown-ups in the bus got up to offer her a seat: *they* didn't look a bit tired. I'll fall over any moment now, she thought, closing her eyes and trying to faint. It was a pity she couldn't manage it. How did you inform grown-ups that you were feeling tired and weak? She couldn't actually say: Dear sir, kindly move your fat bottom up a bit, I'm a tired child just about to fall down in a faint and am absolutely exhausted after four strenuous hours of school, one of them with Mr. Weissensteiner the well-known slavedriver who expects you to know dates by heart in history lessons.

Mari stood on tiptoe, heaving a slight sigh now and then and strap-hanging from one of the leather loops put there so that children and young women didn't fall down in a faint when middle-aged gentlemen would not stand up for them.

"End of the line, change here for the Number 10," croaked the loudspeaker. Mari got off, along with a crowd of other schoolchildren. She straightened her sweater, changed her bag over to the other arm and set off down Nissel Street. Past the bench, past the butcher's where Granny used to beg shamelessly for sausage scraps, saying they were "for the dog" when she was really going to make them into sausage dumplings, past the optician's with its display of spectacle frames, past the greengrocer's selling fruit from all over the world, past the radio repair shop that didn't seem to repair many radios but had a window full of television sets.

A sports car came racing along. Mari leaped to safety on the other side of the road. She had reached the café.

Mari went in, feeling breathless because she had run so fast. She could smell her favorite smell inside; freshly baked bread. Mari drew in deep breaths of it, like a fresh air fiend up in the mountains. Then she looked around for Mrs. Panacek. The front of the place was a bakery; the back was the café, and there was Mrs. Panacek, sitting at the back of the room with the safety of a corner behind her, and facing the door, sitting at a table for one. She was looking up at the ceiling.

"She hasn't moved for the last hour," a nervous voice whispered behind Mari.

"Who hasn't?" asked a second, impatient voice.

"That woman there," said the nervous speaker.

Mari turned around. "That," she told the waitress, "is Mrs. Panacek."

"Is it?" said the girl, bewildered.

"My bill, please," someone called, and the waitress automatically took the heavy black folder out of the pocket of her pink apron with an elegant and practiced gesture, flicking it open like a conjuror with a pack of cards.

"Here I am, Mrs. Panacek!" said Mari. "Is this chair free? Thanks," she added, taking one of the spindly little chairs from the next table over to Mrs. Panacek's.

Slowly, Mrs. Panacek's gaze left the ceiling. "Hello," she croaked. And she coughed, the way people cough when it's a long time since they last made use of their vocal cords.

"Well, shall we go?" asked Mari. Nice as the front part, the bakery, smelled, the air was thick and smoky here at the back.

Mrs. Panacek nodded eagerly.

"Have you paid?" Mari cast a quick glance at the table. She couldn't see the twenty-schilling note.

Mrs. Panacek shook her head. Then, with an air of great secrecy, she lifted her coffee cup. The twenty-schilling note was lying underneath it, folded very small.

"Right," said Mari. She tried to attract the waitress's attention a couple of times, in vain. "Hi!"

Mrs. Panacek bent down and pulled up her red stocking, which had slipped down to her ankle. "You ought to change your clothes," remarked Mari, wrinkling her nose. And you ought to have a wash, too, she thought, but she didn't say so. She paid. She wanted to get out into the fresh air.

"Now what?" Mari asked. Once they were outside, Mrs. Panacek stood looking at the toes of her shoes. "I know: *you* don't know either." Mari sighed.

She had been pushing the thought of Mrs. Panacek out of her mind all morning: at school, in the bus, on the way to the café. All she knew was that she just couldn't take Mrs. Panacek back to the Home. Mari imagined dreadful things happening to Mrs. Panacek there: beatings, thumbscrews, burning at the stake, red-hot pincers. And not being allowed to watch television.

Mari had a good idea. One that wouldn't last them more than two or three hours, but better than no idea at all. "Would you like to go to the zoo?"

"Yes, let's go to the zoo."

Mari took Mrs. Panacek's arm. At a slow and leisurely pace they went down Nissel Street and over the Kennedy Bridge. When they reached the ice-cream parlor, Mari said encouragingly, "Wait a moment—I'll be right back." She went in and came back three minutes later carrying two large tubs of ice cream with whipped cream topping.

Mrs. Panacek enjoyed it. "Cold," she said.

"Yes, it would be," said Mari, and they both laughed. Peaceably eating ice cream, they headed for the park gates.

It was quiet in the park. Not many people came to Schönbrunn at this time of day: the young people were still at work, and though the children were out of school, they'd be at home doing their homework. No one had time to go to the park except the old-age pensioners, who walked down the long pathways on their own, hoping to meet someone they knew or even someone they didn't know. Some of them did not want to meet anyone at all; they just wanted to watch the birds pecking up the food they had brought.

It was even emptier in the zoo itself, which was in the middle of the park. A morose keeper gave Mari and Mrs. Panacek one yellow and one blue tear-off ticket.

The red-bottomed baboon was howling. Mari made faces at him. She and Mrs. Panacek leaned on the green metal bar that is supposed to protect visitors from the wild animals.

[76]

Then Mrs. Panacek removed her hand from the bar. Mari didn't realize what was going on until she heard a splashing sound. There was Mrs. Panacek, squatting over the gravel, with her skirt up, making a little stream of water.

Mari looked anxiously around. She saw a child squatting down opposite them, outside the little yellow newsstand, which was closed at the moment. A toddler. The toddler was squatting in exactly the same position as Mrs. Panacek, with her own skirt up, making a splashing noise.

The little girl was eyeball to eyeball with Mrs. Panacek. She gurgled with delight. So did Mrs. Panacek.

The toddler's mother came running up. "Anni," she called, "Anni! *Good* girl, Anni!" She picked the child up, pulling up her underpants. The little girl looked happily at Mrs. Panacek, still squatting there. The woman put the little girl down and looked angrily at Mrs. Panacek and Mari. She came over to them, pulling little Anni along behind her. Anni looked scared.

"There *are* such things as public toilets!" the woman told Mari, who helplessly shrugged her shoulders.

Mrs. Panacek got to her feet. It was not easy for her to rise from a squatting position quickly at her age.

"Not right in the head, is she?" said the woman, shaking her own head. She spoke more quietly this time; it was not as easy to be angry with Mrs. Panacek on her feet as when she was squatting.

"The little girl did a wee-wee too," said Mrs. Panacek, rather bewildered, looking anxiously at the woman and then smiling at the little girl.

"Come along, Anni."

"It's all right for children," said Mari. Anni stretched out a longing hand to Mrs. Panacek as she was being dragged away, and Mrs. Panacek waved.

Mrs. Panacek looked sad, and Mari felt there must be something wrong with the world if a mother can be pleased with her child for peeing on a gravel path, but horrified to see a nice old lady do the same thing. Why didn't Mari simply squat down and do it too?

"Some time or other they break you of the habit," she murmured to herself.

"Break you of what habit?" asked Mrs. Panacek.

"The habit of—of"— Mari searched for the right words— "being little," she said at last. "Sometimes I feel as old as—" Mari stopped. It suddenly struck her as odd for an eleven-year-old to be saying how old she felt.

"Yes," said Mrs. Panacek thoughtfully. "They break you of all those things. Being happy. And sad. And little. They don't like it, no; it scares them. Everything has to be just so. Your clothes and your bedside table, and meals and life. Most of all they're scared to be them."

"Scared to be them?"

"Scared to be their own selves," said Mrs. Panacek. "You should be your own self, so that nobody else is just like you. I'm the only Mrs. Panacek in the world. No, they don't like you to be your own self."

"Who doesn't?" asked Mari, interested.

"Everybody! The government, teachers, the ladies in the public toilets, the butchers, all of them. My son-in-law."

"Teachers, yes!" Mari knew about that from sad experience. "My parents won't let me do what I want either. Granny certainly won't."

"You can't work once you're your own self," said Mrs. Panacek sadly. "I can't work anymore, because I'm so very much my own self."

She spread out her arms like two wings, and set one foot cautiously in front of the other as she walked along the gravel path. "Mind you, don't fall!" she said. She compressed her lips until they were very thin, she was concentrating so hard.

Mari laughed, and walked the imaginary tightrope after

her, closing her eyes so that she could feel what her legs were doing better. Now she could hear the sound of the audience murmuring below her and the drums rolling in the circus orchestra.

"Ow!" Mari clutched her stomach. She had collided head on with a child. "Wait!" she called. Mrs. Panacek the tightrope dancer was already two cages ahead of her, walking her invisible rope.

"*Waaah!*" roared Mari as loud as she could, and then she flung herself on one of the lawns labeled KEEP OFF THE GRASS and buried her head in her arms. Some perfectly ghastly kind of retribution ought to descend upon her now. Maybe lightning would strike, or Granny would come around the next corner.

Nothing happened. Mari sat up, relieved. "Crazy!" she said, breathless as well as relieved. She had red spots on both cheeks. "It's great! It's crazy! I like tightrope walking. *And* shouting really loud!"

Mrs. Panacek came back, and sat down on the grass beside Mari. And suddenly, while Mrs. Panacek was pulling up blades of grass, looking for a four-leaf clover, Mari knew what to do: she wouldn't kill any more time in the zoo with Mrs. Panacek; she'd go to see Father. She couldn't go to Mother's office; they didn't like Mother to have visitors there. But Father might be able to help Mrs. Panacek. After all, he was forever saying she could bring him her problems anytime, and even if he sometimes seemed impatient, he'd always listen.

"We're going to see my father," said Mari, pulling the surprised Mrs. Panacek up from the grass. "Come on, get up!" she said impatiently.

They set off on foot. It would not take them more than a quarter of an hour to reach the television studio, where Father worked.

10

THREE faces looked up from their newspapers. Mr. Heininger, head of the props department, Mr. Bayer and Mr. Kaminski.

"Hello, it's Wagner's little girl!" said Mr. Bayer.

"Is my father here?" asked Mari shyly. She was afraid of Mr. Bayer, who was as broad as an old kitchen dresser and as tall as a church steeple.

"He'll be back soon." Mr. Heininger lowered his newspaper. "I just sent him out to the junk shop to look for some walking sticks."

"Oh," said Mari.

The property men all knew Mari, but not Mrs. Panacek. They were probably asking themselves how such a bedraggled old woman could have got into the television studio without a pass, what with the strict antiterrorist precautions in force. In fact, Mari and Mrs. Panacek had had no trouble at all getting in. The glazed booth where the porter was supposed to sit was empty, so they had simply walked past the barriers and crossed the reception area without being noticed either.

"Your granny?" asked Mr. Kaminski kindly.

"Just a friend of mine," said Mari.

But Mr. Kaminski was already deep in his crossword puzzle again. No one in here ever overworked; you could practically smell that in the air. Mari looked past the barred door, which was standing ajar, into the props rooms: a wonderland crammed with old-fashioned objects.

"Go on in," said Mr. Kaminski, seeing Mari's wistful glance. He made a vague gesture. "Have a look if you like. You know your way around."

Mari beamed. "Come on," she said, taking Mrs. Panacek's hand. "Come on, let's go in." The barred door squealed. Mari had seen that Mrs. Panacek was wary of the property men reading their papers in the office. "Don't worry," she said. "Your son-in-law isn't here."

Mrs. Panacek heaved a sigh of relief and gave Mari a grateful look.

They found themselves among the lamps. Mrs. Panacek stood and stared. The shelves here were all filled with lovely, elegant lampshades. "That one's mine!" cried Mrs. Panacek in delight, seizing upon a pink and rather dusty lamp. "It stands by my bed, and Karl has one like it on *his* bedside table!"

"I'm afraid not," said Mari sadly. "It can't be yours. I expect it just looks the same."

"Looks the same, yes." Mrs. Panacek fondled the pink lampshade. "Mine is burnt." She sniffed the lampshade. "This one doesn't smell burnt."

"No," said Mari, still rather sadly. It was sometimes so hard to understand Mrs. Panacek. But Mrs. Panacek was looking sad herself now, so Mari quickly tried to take her mind off the lamps.

"Look—over there!" She pointed to the swords. However,

Mrs. Panacek was not interested in swords, only lamp-shades.

"Here," said Mari. "This way." She walked on, through rows of tall shelves. "Come on, we might find Mrs. Bierbaum in the wardrobe."

Reluctantly, Mrs. Panacek followed Mari. She kept turning to look back at the pink lampshade. Sometimes she stopped, ran her fingers over the dusty switches of the lamps, flipped them on or off—but no light came on. "Useless," muttered Mrs. Panacek, rather annoyed, and wiped her dusty fingers on her skirt. It was so dirty already that a bit more dust made no difference.

The next barred door was open. "There, look at that!" said Mari softly. She stood still, waiting impatiently for Mrs. Panacek to catch up with her.

Costume hanging by costume. Suits of armor leaning up in one corner. Lace-trimmed dresses, shelves full of hats, suits, clown costumes, sailor suits, cowboy outfits.

"Why, if it isn't Marianne. Fancy seeing you!" said Mrs. Bierbaum. "Your dad's not here, though." Mrs. Bierbaum was sitting in the corner behind the racks of suits. She put her sewing down; she was taking in a green dress. "No flesh on 'em, the actresses these days," she said, showing Mari the dress. "I'm always having to take things in and shorten them."

She glanced inquiringly at Mrs. Panacek.

"This is someone Father knows," lied Mari. Well, it was not entirely untrue: he *had* seen her this morning.

"I see." Mrs. Bierbaum went on sewing.

"We'd love to look around," said Mari timidly. "May we?"

"Yes, yes," said Mrs. Bierbaum absently, switching on the little green radio on the table. "But mind you don't disturb anything."

[82]

The place was like a forest: a forest made of clothes. Mrs. Panacek's eyes shone. "Oh, look!" she said reverently, stopping to look at a silk dress. "Such a good piece of stuff."

"*Shh*, keep quiet!" Mari begged her. "Or Mrs. Bierbaum will throw us out—she gets into funny moods. Wouldn't it be fun to dress up?" She giggled. Go on, whispered the little imp that lived inside Mari, do it! No, certainly not, Mari told the imp, and passed the suggestion on to Mrs. Panacek.

"Go on, Mrs. Panacek, try it on!"

Mari was so happy and excited that she was biting her lips quite hard as she helped Mrs. Panacek out of her own dirty clothes. Mrs. Panacek looked no better underneath: her stockings were full of holes, and not very clean either.

"My goodness, what white skin you've got!" said Mari in surprise.

"White skin is a sign of good breeding," Mrs. Panacek told her, keeping an eye on the other end of the gangway.

"I'm sure Mrs. Bierbaum won't come," said Mari, shifting impatiently from one foot to the other.

Mrs. Panacek shook her head. "No, no!" she said.

"Oh, I see." Mari sighed. Mrs. Panacek had not been looking out for Mrs. Bierbaum; she was feeling frightened of her son-in-law again. The murderer who wasn't really a murderer. Mari was gradually coming to understand Mrs. Panacek.

"He can't get in here; he hasn't got a pass," said Mari, hoping Mrs. Panacek wouldn't remember that *they* hadn't had passes either.

"No." Mrs. Panacek beamed in relief. "He hasn't got a pass."

"Put it on!" Mari urged her.

The silk dress crackled as Mrs. Panacek slipped it on. She shivered; silk is cold. The zipper at the back wouldn't go up. Mrs. Panacek was wearing a cotton undershirt.

"I don't suppose they wore underwear like that in the old days," said Mari.

"Oh, yes they did," said Mrs. Panacek. "Not the fine ladies, maybe, but folk like us. We didn't have the money for fine stuff like this."

Mari led Mrs. Panacek over to a big mirror standing between two rows of clothes. "Well?" she asked. "Do you like it?"

"Lovely!" said Mrs. Panacek. "Though pink's not really my color. A hat! I must have a hat!" And Mrs. Panacek bundled her gray hair under the black hat Mari handed her.

"There!" Mrs. Panacek was smiling all over her face. "Very nice." She pirouetted in front of the mirror, looking at herself from all angles. Then she bent down and flapped her hand in the air in front of her red stocking. "Shoo!" she told it, but it did not go away. She sat down on the floor and took off her woollen stockings: a fine lady doesn't wear such things. She carelessly tossed the odd stockings under a clothes rack. Mari prudently retrieved them and put them in her bag.

"Shoes," said Mari. "You need shoes. Stay here and keep quiet."

Mari had to crawl under two clothes racks to get at the shoe shelves, and then she realized she had forgotten to ask Mrs. Panacek her size. "Well, let's say seven," murmured Mari. The sizes were marked on the soles of the shoes, and size seven is about average.

Invisible to Mari, Mrs. Bierbaum turned up the volume of her radio. "The news: when the gong strikes it will be five P.M. Here is the news. . . ."

"Here you are!" Mari had wriggled her way back, and gave Mrs. Panacek a pair of shoes. She had to squeeze her old feet in, but the shoes fitted well enough.

"Great!" said Mari.

"Very nice!" Mrs. Panacek too was pleased with her appearance, and smiled at her reflection in the mirror. "I look like I did in the old days, when I had the shop," she said. "Oh, yes, I always looked as smart as this. Not in the shop, of course, because of my apron. But in the evenings—ah, the evenings!"

"*Ssh!*" whispered Mari. "Not so loud."

"Ah, yes, the evenings!"

Mari was sure Mrs. Bierbaum must have heard, but the newscaster was saying, "And finally, the weather forecast," and there was no sound out of the wardrobe mistress.

Then she heard a man's voice. Father.

"She's over there, Mr. Wagner," said Mrs. Bierbaum, loud and clear. "Getting a big girl, your Marianne is!"

"Mari!" called Father. "Where are you, Mari?"

"Oh, quick, take it off!"

Mari almost pulled the dress off Mrs. Panacek. The end of the zipper broke, and the zipper hung limply down.

"Quick, hang it up!" Mari got Mrs. Panacek into her dirty skirt. "Now your stockings." She got them out of her case.

Father came around the corner.

"Mari!" he cried. "What on earth are you doing?"

Thunderstruck, he stared at Mari and Mrs. Panacek, who was still having trouble with her odd stockings. "Good God, don't say *she's* still with us!" he exclaimed, and then realized that he didn't sound very polite.

"I couldn't do it," said Mari guiltily. "Take her back to the Home, I mean. Father, *please!*"

She stood on tiptoe and whispered, "Please, please!" into Father's ear. She didn't really know what she was asking for, but she thought, "Please, please!" was bound to sound good. Father's ear was cool from the chilly evening air.

"I'll do it tomorrow. Please, Father!"

The stern glance Father so often practiced failed to have

any effect on Mari. He took something out of his pocket. A folded newspaper.

"Here, look at this," he said. He spread the paper out and brought his hand down on it a couple of times. "Look!"

"Where?" asked Mari. She couldn't see anything special on the page, only a huge photograph of a blond young woman with two naked breasts and a winning smile.

"There!" Father's forefinger indicated a few lines beside the naked blonde.

Missing: Seventy-eight-year-old Maria Panacek, an inmate of the Alder Yard Psychiatric Hospital, has been missing for two days. She was last seen wearing a gray skirt, light-colored sweater and one red and one black stocking. She sometimes suffers from loss of memory. Anyone knowing the missing woman's whereabouts is asked to contact the nearest police station, or phone 817-6710.

"They're looking for her," said Father, sounding agitated. "The police are looking for her, you see."

"Yes," said Mari, disappointed. Her disappointment was because the newspaper thought Mrs. Panacek was only worth eight lines. Eight short little lines that almost nobody would read. But blond Vanessa from Australia, of the astonishing breasts, took up almost the whole page, and *she* wasn't missing, or sick; she was well and happy with a whole page of newspaper to herself. Whereas poor Mrs. Panacek, who was frightened and didn't have a proper home anymore, only got those eight lines. Mari thought the world was not just unfair, but very hard to understand.

"Don't show it to her, or she may get scared," Mari whispered into her father's ear. Sighing, he folded the newspaper and put it back in his pocket.

"Well," he said, "*something* has to be done!"

"Father, please!"

Mari adopted her pleading expression, which, unlike Father's stern one, almost always worked.

Father looked uneasily away from Mari, staring through Mrs. Panacek. Mrs. Panacek was still battling with her stockings. "Oh, go and help her," said Father impatiently. "And meanwhile I'll call Mother."

He went off. Mrs. Panacek was red in the face. Was she feeling embarrassed, annoyed or just excited?

"It's all right, Mrs. Panacek," Mari said soothingly. "You needn't be frightened of my father. He's nice, he'd never hurt anyone, honestly. Look, he's calling Mother now."

Father was standing by the public phone at the far end of the big room. Mari could see him gesticulating, but she couldn't hear what he was saying. He shifted from foot to foot, rocked up and down on his toes, and scratched his left calf with his right shoe, through his trousers. He also scratched his ear with his free hand. He drew invisible patterns on the wall with one finger. Then he hung up.

Father came back. "Tonight," he said. "Just for one night. We'll have to take her back tomorrow."

"Who's *we*?"

"Well, you and Mother; I won't have time."

"Okay," said Mari, a little peevishly, but also a little pleased. Yet again she had gained more time. Mrs. Panacek had gained more time.

"Thank you, thank you!" said Mrs. Panacek, suddenly beaming at Father and casting him into confusion. Not knowing Mrs. Panacek as well as Mari did, he didn't know when she was listening and when she wasn't, or how much of what one said she took in.

"You're welcome," said Father, staring at a small round hole in the floor covering.

[87]

All this time Mrs. Panacek had been looking at Mari very lovingly, so that Mari felt herself go warm inside. Discovering that someone really likes you is nice, Mari thought. She went over to Mrs. Panacek and took her arm, which sometimes hung down beside her body as if it didn't belong to her, and laid it round her own small shoulders. "Come on, Mrs. Panacek, we're going now," she said. She nuzzled her head into the hollow of Mrs. Panacek's shoulder for a moment, and then started walking, so that Mrs. Panacek had to go with her whether she liked or not. Father went ahead of them.

11

FATHER opened the car door.

"I've got to go to Lustig's before we go home," he said. "He's got a scrap heap in the basement where I might find some stuff I need."

Mari nodded and helped Mrs. Panacek into the car: not very easy, since the car only had two doors, and the back seat was full of odds and ends. Mrs. Panacek's dirty skirt disappeared inside. Mari wondered briefly whether to sit in front with Father, but then she got in the back too, so that Mrs. Panacek wouldn't be scared there on her own. Also because she was sure that otherwise Father would keep looking anxiously in the rear-view mirror, to see if Mrs. Panacek was still there and acting normally, so far as you can expect a mad person to act normally.

By *normally* Father would mean sitting quietly and not ranting and raving. Mari knew that Mrs. Panacek wouldn't do that anyway, because she was quite calm at the moment and she felt warm. When she was agitated, or about to get either agitated or scared, she felt different: her face and hands were cold.

Father started the car and drove past the barriers. The porter (the one who didn't keep too close an eye on the television studio) touched his cap as they passed.

"Lustig's place is near the city's center," sighed Father. "And it's rush hour too!"

The traffic was all right here on the outskirts of the city, but the closer they came to the center the thicker it was. Soon there was no point in even thinking about moving forward; they were stuck in a jam. Father perspired, swore and muttered crossly. Mari didn't mind; she looked at the back lights of the other cars or counted the noses of the people in the ones next to them. She made a face at an Alsatian dog which was barking inaudibly. It looked as if it were yawning very fast over and over again.

Mrs. Panacek had leaned back and was watching Father's hands clutching the steering wheel, changing gear, impatiently tapping the empty passenger seat.

The traffic started to crawl and then to move—jerkily, but at least they were moving forward.

Father wiped the sweat from his brow as they drew near their destination, and muttered something about the increased risk of coronaries these days and the idiocy of living in the city instead of out in the country.

"Why don't you go away before it's too late?" whispered Mrs. Panacek. She had not uttered a sound during the whole drive, and Father jumped. He had almost forgotten she was there in the back.

"Before it's too late?" he asked, shifting uneasily in his seat. "Too late for what?"

"Everything," said Mrs. Panacek. "Before it's all over. Life, I mean."

Openmouthed, Mari stared at Mrs. Panacek helplessly.

"Life is running past," said Mrs. Panacek, leaning forward to Father. "There are some people who steal life," she said, close to his ear. "They steal other people's time."

Mari couldn't help laughing. "You can't steal time! Or life either. Our lives are our own."

"No, no," sighed Mrs. Panacek, leaning back again. "They belong to other people." And she looked sad as she spoke.

Father was searching for a parking place. "Mrs. Panacek is right," he said. Mari was bewildered; Father too sounded sad now. He put the car into reverse, with a crunch of gears. "We're nothing but fools," he said, glancing back over his right shoulder. "Work, work, work, that's all we do."

"And kind regards from the transmission," Mari said—a remark Mother often made when Father clashed the gears. Father repeated, "Nothing but fools."

"Fools are caught, but the mad are free," said Mrs. Pan-acek happily, looking out of the window.

"You're not really free in the Home," said Mari. Mrs. Panacek turned her head, mildly surprised.

"Not that sort of free," she said peaceably. "Free in our heads."

"Hm. I don't know," said Father dubiously, but he wasn't really listening anymore. His thoughts were somewhere else, perhaps at Mr. Lustig's where they were going.

Then Mrs. Panacek suddenly turned white as a sheet, and her nose looked pinched. She stretched out her arm, right in front of Mari's face, and pointed excitedly through the back window.

"There . . . th-there . . ." she said, stammering like a toddler.

"What is it?" asked the bewildered Mari, taking Mrs. Panacek's arm.

"There . . . there. . . ."

"Good Lord, look how she's trembling!" said Father in alarm. Mrs. Panacek was indeed trembling all over.

Mari looked the way she was pointing and saw a shop with a sign over it in large letters, saying: M. PANACEK—FISH.

"There!" Mari told Father, getting worked up herself. "Father, look!"

"M. Panacek—Fish," Father read. He got the point at once. "Is that your shop, then?" he asked Mrs. Panacek.

Mrs. Panacek couldn't nod; she was trembling like an aspen. "Hold on to her," Father told Mari. Mari put her arms round Mrs. Panacek and talked soothingly to her, the way she had once seen a man do in a film. There was a woman crying her head off in this film, and the man took her in his arms saying, "It'll all be all right, it'll all be all right," in a monotonously high-pitched and rapid voice, as if he were trying to hypnotize her.

Mari wished she could hypnotize Mrs. Panacek. "It'll all be all right," she whispered, "it'll all be all right. Yes, yes, it's your shop, but you needn't get upset. The rest of them have to do the work now. You don't have to take fish out of cold water and get your hands freezing anymore, or wear an apron with blood on it, or get up early in the morning to see to everything. . . . It'll all be all right . . . all right, all right."

Mari stopped. An idea had occurred to her.

"Is *he* in there?" she asked.

Mrs. Panacek did not reply, but she was calmer now.

"Is he in there? Your son-in-law?" Mari asked again. "The murderer?" she added, very quietly.

Instead of replying, Mrs. Panacek sobbed aloud.

Mari quickly put her hand into Mrs. Panacek's skirt pocket. She knew the pills were in there, and Mrs. Panacek had said they were to calm her down. "Here," said Mari, handing them to her. "There isn't any water, I'm afraid."

"Only one," said Mrs. Panacek, dropping one tablet on the car floor and trying to swallow the other, with some difficulty.

"You'll have to get it down somehow without water," said Mari. "Maybe it'll help." I hope so, she thought.

Father got out of the car, exchanging a glance with Mari. He looked like Zorro the avenger of the disinherited as he made for the fish shop with a swaggering cowboy stride.

Mrs. Panacek laid her head on one side.

"I'm going to sleep now," she said, and stopped trembling.

"Yes, do that," said Mari lovingly, thinking: I wish I could drop off to sleep just like that. For in only a minute Mrs. Panacek was breathing deeply, slowly and peacefully.

Mari sat there thinking. It had begun to rain. They were cozy in the car; the engine crackled as it cooled off, and raindrops pattered on the car roof.

Warily, Mari got out, after making sure Mrs. Panacek really was fast asleep.

She wanted to go into the fishmonger's too. She wanted to know what the place where Mrs. Panacek had spent almost half her life looked like. And she wanted to know what was keeping Father in there with Mrs. Panacek's daughter and son-in-law so long. Perhaps they were fighting. Mari imagined her father lying among the carp covered with blood, and a seven-foot-tall murderer, strong as a bear, trampling him underfoot. . . .

Brr! Mari pushed these silly thoughts out of her head. She pressed her nose to the car window once again, from the outside. Mrs. Panacek was quite still.

"I'll only be a minute," she whispered to the car, and then ran across the road.

The fishmonger's was full of tired men and women: mostly women. Behind the carp tank, just as Mari had imagined it, stood a big strong man whom she disliked on sight. That must be him—the son-in-law. He didn't look like a murderer, however. Mari thought he simply looked stupid.

On the other side of the shop, which had a glass display case full of bowls of prepared salads, stood a woman wearing a blue-and-white overall. She was pale and looked tired, and she kept pushing back a lock of hair from her forehead: fair hair with a slight reddish tinge to it from the fish blood.

Father was talking to the woman.

The place stank of fish. It made Mari feel rather sick, but she pulled herself together. She made her way through the crowd toward Father. The fair woman was looking anxiously at the big strong man the whole time, wondering if he would see that she was talking to a stranger who was not buying anything. There was a young girl assistant at the checkout counter.

When Father noticed the woman keeping a wary eye on her husband he began buying things at random.

"I'll have half a pound of herring salad. The same of Waldorf salad. Er—some coleslaw. Some tomato salad. Six ounces of crabmeat." Mari wondered who was going to eat all this, and who was paying for it. She reached Father at last and slipped her hand into his.

He nodded to her briefly. "The old lady's badly upset," she heard him say. "Your husband must have put the fear of God into her! Why does he go to Alder Yard anyway, when he knows she's afraid of him?"

"I don't know," said the woman helplessly, piling coleslaw into a plastic carton, weighing it, fishing some out with a spoon and weighing it again. "He wouldn't hurt her," said Mrs. Panacek's daughter. "He only wanted to visit her, that's all. I'm sure he didn't know she'd be so scared. He wouldn't hurt a fly."

"No?" said Father sharply. He raised his voice. "You're afraid of him yourself."

The woman glanced anxiously at her husband, who didn't notice. "He gets scared of things too. I'm weaker, that's all."

"You mean he beats you?" said Father, horrified.

"It's just his way," said the woman. "Will there be anything else?"

"I'll have a carp," said Father quickly. And he added, "You could at least try to see he doesn't terrorize the old lady."

"There's no need for Mother to be frightened," said the woman. "One carp. Is that all?"

"Yes," said Father grimly. Mrs. Panacek's daughter wrote down quite a large sum of money with the stub of a pencil on a greasy piece of wrapping paper.

"Pay the cashier, please."

As Father and Mari were making their way through the crowd of people toward the checkout counter, she called after them, "I'll have a word with him." Father glanced back at her. "Good," he muttered to himself. Mari saw the woman wipe her brow. Father paid.

Then, suddenly, Mrs. Panacek's daughter was there beside them. "Thank you," she said, pressing another package into Father's hand. "It's not my fault," she said. "The court said Mom wasn't fit to manage her own affairs. The shop belongs to my husband now—the court awarded it to him, he had a lawyer and all. Because Mom was sick, you see."

"I see," said Father.

Mari spoke up. "She's still sick."

"I know," said the woman wearily. "You'll take her back to the Home, won't you?"

She went back to her counter. She did not look happy.

"Come on, Mari." Father took a firmer grip on Mari's hand and left the fishmonger's, with one last black look at the son-in-law, who was looking at him in bafflement. Then they were standing on the street.

"What a thing, what a thing!" said Father crossly, marching over to the car. One of his hands was holding Mari's, the other was holding a carrier bag full of salads and one carp, which he had paid for, plus the other package, which had been a present and turned out to contain three more big, fat, rich carp. Who on earth was going to eat them?

"What a thing!" Father muttered again. He stopped, hugged Mari, and gave her a kiss on the end of her nose. "Do you realize just how lucky we are?" he asked. He did not wait for an answer, but propelled Mari toward the car.

"I think I'll give Lustig's a miss for today," he said, starting the engine, and he drove straight home with Mari, the sleeping Mrs. Panacek and a sense of righteous anger. Apparently Mari was the only person to notice that he went through a red light, but she did not say anything; she was just glad there hadn't been an accident. That didn't bear thinking of.

12

EVEN though Granny was there at home, it was *not* fish for supper. There was a lovely smell of roast pork.

Granny was standing very upright by the kitchen cupboard, examining Mrs. Panacek as if she were a strange being from another planet. "This is Mrs. Panacek, Mama," Mother told Granny, performing the introduction very correctly. She was already wishing she had not asked Granny to come along for the evening as a kind of specialist in old ladies. Mother herself did not know much about the psychology of old ladies, but now she was beginning to suspect that Granny might know even less. As a specialist in old ladies, in fact, Granny was hopeless. Mari could have told Mother that if only she'd been asked.

The table was laid for five, looking very pretty, with the white damask cloth that Granny used to say should be kept for Sundays, special occasions, birthdays and visits from important people. There was much pulling out of chairs.

"Fish." Father put the packet of carp in the refrigerator.

"Splendid," said Mother. "We'll eat it tomorrow."

"Very sensible!" said Granny approvingly. "Always buy in advance. Fish is good for you. Aren't you going to give her a plastic mat?"

Mari turned red. "No, thank you, Granny, I don't need a plastic mat," she said, just to embarrass her grandmother. She knew quite well Granny had meant Mrs. Panacek and not herself.

"Just half a dumpling for me, please," said Father quickly. Mother neatly bisected the dumpling with a piece of thread so it would keep its nice shape.

"Thanks," said Father.

Granny began to eat, in silence.

"What about you, Mrs. Panacek?" asked Mother. "A whole dumpling or a half?"

"A whole one, if I may," said Mrs. Panacek very politely. Granny looked at her in surprise. What was going on in Granny's head? She must be in a state of utter bewilderment; she would certainly have imagined a madwoman would be quite different! A sort of Fury, gnashing her teeth and slaughtering little children with a bloody knife.

"Well, do start, everyone," said Father.

They did. Granny was a little ashamed because she was the only one who already *had* started, and her slice of pork showed it.

There was a loud, lip-smacking noise.

Granny looked up from her plate. Mrs. Panacek was smacking her lips. She had put down her knife and was concentrating on her meat, which was not particularly tender, holding the large slice up to her mouth on her fork. It hovered in the air, and gravy dropped on and beside her plate. Mrs. Panacek attacked the meat with her teeth.

Granny frowned—no, glowered!

Then Mari copied Mrs. Panacek, tearing at her own slice of meat with her teeth and smacking her lips loudly.

"Mari!" snapped Grandmother.

Mari closed her eyes for a moment, waiting for her parents to come down on her like a ton of bricks—but nothing happened. Father cleared his throat and began attacking his dumpling wildly and messily. Mother bit back her laughter. She got up, went over to the stove, fetched the pan and slapped a helping of sauerkraut on her plate so carelessly that the gravy splashed around. Granny's face went pale and pinched; she muttered something about everyone being against her, and stuck her little finger out from the side of her fork, which was apparently supposed to be the height of good manners. Father laughed. Mother laughed.

Mrs. Panacek went on eating. She was enjoying the meal; she didn't mind how her table manners looked.

"One does *not* eat that way!" Granny pronounced.

"No?" said Father. "But we're enjoying it this way."

Mother took her white napkin out of her real silver engraved napkin ring, pressed it to her mouth and dashed out.

"I dare say she feels sick," said Granny, with satisfaction.

However, she was wrong; Mother was just outside the door, in fits of laughter. Mari, helpless with laughter herself, joined her.

"Oh, no, oh, no, oh, no!" moaned Mother. "Ha, ha, ha!"

Father, preserving his masculine dignity, sat up very correctly and said he thought it was about time to be serious.

"My own opinion exactly," said Granny.

Mrs. Panacek was still noisily enjoying her meal. "A napkin, Mrs. Panacek?" Granny eventually asked when Mrs. Panacek leaned back with her fingers and lips all greasy. Mari came back into the room, grinning.

"No, thank you," said Mrs. Panacek pleasantly, wiping her mouth on her hands.

"Have this," said Mari, holding up the napkin, because the back of Mrs. Panacek's hand was quite shiny now.

"Yes, thank you!" said Mrs. Panacek. She was happy enough to take it from Mari; not from Granny. Mrs. Panacek was very quick to notice whether you really liked her or not.

Father cleared the table—not entirely of his own free will, but after a reproachful look from Mother. Granny sat bolt upright at the kitchen table waiting for the coffee that didn't come, because no one had thought of making it. Mother went to fetch family photographs and spread them out in front of Mrs. Panacek. Among them were pictures of Mari as a baby. "And who do you think *that* is?" Mother asked. Mrs. Panacek could not guess. "Mari!"

"Oh, Mari!" said Mrs. Panacek reverently, holding the photograph at arm's length. "Mari. So little then!"

Mari was amazed, as she always was when she saw old photographs of herself. To think how fast time went by! Especially when it went by without your noticing. For instance, Mari had never really noticed herself growing. At least, she'd never been woken in the night by a sudden spurt of growth, to find that her pajama pants were suddenly too short.

"I once grew too," said Mrs. Panacek solemnly.

"No!" said Father. "Who'd have thought it?"

Everyone laughed except for Granny and Mrs. Panacek, who was a good-humored person but didn't understand irony. Maybe she never had. So she repeated earnestly, "Oh, yes. I *did* grow once."

Father patted her shoulder and explained that he'd only been joking.

"Yes, yes," said Mrs. Panacek, at something of a loss, and Granny shrugged her shoulders and began cleaning her fingernails with a fork. "*That's* not very nice, either," said Mari, and Granny turned as red as a bottle of ketchup.

Mother not only got more photographs out of more cupboards, but fetched all her oil paintings off the top of the living-room cupboard. "Only a hobby, I'm afraid," she said, showing them to Mrs. Panacek.

Father thought Mother could make a career of painting, but Mother said it wouldn't be nearly secure enough. "I don't have the right artistic temperament," she used to say. However, she felt flattered that Father believed she could be a professional painter.

Mari didn't think her pictures were anything great; you couldn't tell what they were supposed to show. That, Mother had explained, is called "abstract painting." When she painted a vase of flowers that didn't look like a vase of flowers but like—well, like something else, that was an abstract. However, Mother didn't paint vases of flowers anyway, on principle, or flowers, seascapes, sunsets or deer in the forest. Mother painted feelings. So she said.

At the moment she was showing Mrs. Panacek a picture of green feelings.

Mrs. Panacek liked it. "Oh, it's so green!" she said appreciatively. No one could have denied that, but evidently when Mrs. Panacek said "so green" she meant the same as Mother did, but Mother was not like Mrs. Panacek. So far as painting went, however, they seemed to share the same tastes.

"I like painting too," said Mrs. Panacek.

"Really?" asked Mari.

"Yes," said Mrs. Panacek. "I have some drawings at the Home."

Mother interrupted them by producing another green painting. She was in full swing now; once she began showing you her pictures she was unstoppable. The second green picture really *was* lovely. Even Mari thought so, though she wouldn't have described the green pictures just as "so green," herself. She might have said something like, "Green dot setting behind the earth." Yes, why not? It was a sudden idea she'd have liked to tell Mother right away, if Granny hadn't roped her in to make coffee. And while she was filling the coffee mill with beans, Mari thought that if it was really her feelings Mother was painting, they must be pretty crazy feelings! Maybe just as crazy as Mrs. Panacek's. The only difference being that Mother kept her feelings for weekends, while Mrs. Panacek had hers seven days a week.

"Now for a game of Parcheesi!" Father asked Granny to go and look for the board.

Granny protested; she did not want to play Parcheesi. She wrinkled up her nose as she passed Mrs. Panacek.

"Wouldn't you like a bath, dear Mrs. Hanazweck?" she said, pretending to have forgotten Mrs. Panacek's name, although in fact she remembered it perfectly well. Granny could be spiteful.

"Mrs. *Panacek*," said Mari. "You know she's called Panacek!"

"Oh, dear, I'm afraid I forgot," said Granny.

But Mother seized upon the bath idea. "That's a good notion," she said. "Yes, a wonderful idea! We'll run you a lovely, warm, scented bubble bath, Mrs. Panacek! A bubble bath scented with sandalwood!"

Gleefully, Mother clapped her hands like a child, and Mari laughed with pleasure. Mother went into the bathroom and ran hot water, squeezing in some drops of yellow cream. "After that I'll find you something else to wear," she called out from the bathroom. Her voice sounded hollow.

"That's a good idea too," Mari told Mrs. Panacek. "Then you'll have something clean to wear when you go back to the Home tomorrow." She saw the anxious expression come over Mrs. Panacek's face again. "Don't worry," said Mari, quick to reassure her. "Father's seen to everything. He's made sure your son-in-law won't go there anymore. Father can fix *anything*."

Mrs. Panacek believed in the unlimited influence of Mari's father. Mari stood up, rather uncertainly, and went off in search of the scent of sandalwood.

"Why are you shaking your head all the time?" Mari asked Granny.

"Ah, well!" said Granny, sniffily. "Ah, well!" She couldn't seem to think of anything else to say. Acting as if nothing had happened, she asked Father sweetly, "Well, and where do you keep the Parcheesi board?"

There was condensation misting up the bathroom mirror. Mrs. Panacek stood in the bathroom looking rather lost and helpless. So did Mother. Mrs. Panacek began to undress.

"Well, we'll leave you alone," said Mother, embarrassed, but Mrs. Panacek just went on taking her clothes off. She was quite used to undressing in front of other people; there was not much privacy in the Home. Mother tested the bath-water temperature once again with her hand, so that Mrs. Panacek wouldn't scald herself, and then shooed Mari out, following herself.

"Give us a shout if you need anything," she told Mrs. Panacek as she closed the bathroom door from the outside.

After five minutes in the kitchen with Granny, who was still stiff as a poker, Mari decided to take Mrs. Panacek a drink in the bathroom. She found Mrs. Panacek sitting in the bathtub, her eyes closed, covered in foam. She even had foam on the end of her nose, in her ears and on her cheeks and her eyelids. Luckily the sandalwood-scented bubble bath was not the sort that stings the eyes, but had been intended for children. The bottle said, "No More Tears!"

"Lovely!" said Mrs. Panacek, beaming. "It's not such fun bathing at the Home. We don't have foam there, only water."

"Oh, then you must take some bubble bath back with

you," said Mari. She set about collecting all the little sample bottles of bubble bath and oil from the bathroom cupboard and put them beside the big bottle. She must remember them in the morning. "No problems there," Mari murmured.

She fished the red bath tray out from behind the toilet, put it over the bathtub, and placed a big glass of cranberry juice on it, right in front of Mrs. Panacek's nose.

Mrs. Panacek was obviously thirsty; she drank greedily. The water was hot, and Mrs. Panacek's cheeks were red with heat and excitement beneath the foam.

Three quarters of an hour later, Mrs. Panacek was sitting at the living-room table in Father's striped bathrobe, with cold cream rubbed into her face. Mother had just dried her hair with the hair dryer, shaping it into nice waves. A dress Mother no longer wore was draped over a chair. It fitted Mrs. Panacek all right.

"But I want to pay for it," she insisted. Mother was going to refuse, but then she thought that if it mattered to Mrs. Panacek to pay for the dress, then she'd let her.

"She has her pride," Mother whispered to Mari.

"A six!" shouted Father triumphantly from underneath the table.

"Anyone can say that," said Mari indignantly. "You're just pretending!" But the dice really had thrown a six when Father threw it and it fell under the table; how could he help it if the table was too small?

Even Granny had to suppress a smile, though she never took her eyes off Mrs. Panacek's coffee cup.

However, it wasn't Mrs. Panacek who did something clumsy, it was Mother, who got so annoyed with Father that she hit the table, and unfortunately, in so doing, also hit the saucer sitting under the cup that held her coffee. There was coffee all over Mother's skirt and the tablecloth. Granny frowned. Mari was happy enough, though, because she and her red markers were winning. Mrs. Panacek was in third place. "Go on, Mrs. Panacek, get Granny in the eye!" Mari encouraged her.

Granny turned red, and Mrs. Panacek said earnestly, "No, no, she hasn't done anything to hurt me!" Granny turned even redder. "Impossible! Your behavior is simply impossible!" she told Mari, shaking her head. "And as for *you*," she added, turning to Mari's parents, "you just sit there as if nothing was wrong."

"Except that this horrible man keeps getting ahead of me on the board!" said Mother, kicking Father's shin under the table.

"Ouch!" said Father. "Are you crazy?"

Granny tut-tutted, and said she was no longer surprised by her granddaughter's appalling upbringing. "This is no way to behave," said Granny. "*No* way to behave!"

Mrs. Panacek plucked at Granny's sleeve.

"Yes? What is it?" Granny unwillingly turned her head.

"Your family is being funny," Mrs. Panacek told her kindly. "They're not really quarreling! They like each other."

"I suppose *you* are a good judge of that," said Granny, turning her eyes heavenward.

But as Mrs. Panacek still hadn't got the hang of irony, she only nodded and said, rather pleased, that yes, she had always been a good judge of such things.

"I've won!" shouted Father.

"Idiot!" said Mother, and then she gave him a big kiss.

"Too bad," said Mari. "You've lost, Mrs. Panacek. You're not cross, are you?"

"Me? No!" Mrs. Panacek beamed. "No, I'm not cross. I don't ever want to be cross again!"

"And you might take note of *that*, dear Grandmother," Father told his mother-in-law.

"Rosi!" protested Granny, summoning her daughter to

her aid. "Rosi!" Mari thought Granny sometimes bleated like a sheep. "Rosi," bleated the sheep, "kindly tell your husband—"

But Mother was not listening; she was pouring a little more milk into Mrs. Panacek's coffee cup.

"I see!" said Granny, pushing back her chair. She did not say what she saw; instead, she went out of the room and came back with her coat.

"I'm going now," she announced.

"Sleep well," said Father peaceably.

"Lovely to see you," said Mother politely.

"Good-bye, dear Mrs. Meier," said Mrs. Panacek kindly.

This was too much for Granny. "Turning out your own flesh and blood!" she spat. "Harboring homeless strangers instead. No family feeling!"

And then Granny stalked out, slamming the door behind her so hard that bits of plaster crumbled off the wall, especially just above the door where there had been a piece missing for quite some time.

"A strong exit, yes, what I'd call a very strong exit," said Father indignantly, picking up the markers and the dice.

"I'll have to have a word with her next time I see her," Mother said to herself out loud. "But I don't want to be in a bad mood today. Another game, Mrs. Panacek?"

And they sat playing Parcheesi until midnight, by which time Mari was asleep in her chair. She had won four times, but Mother had won most of the games and was slightly tipsy, because Father had opened his birthday cognac. Mother decided to put Mari to bed.

"Please!" Mrs. Panacek pushed Mother aside. "Please may I?"

Very carefully, Mrs. Panacek put her arms under Mari,

picked her up with a grunt, and staggered through the doorway. Father was holding the door open for her. She was really much too small to carry someone of Mari's weight, but neither Mother nor Father could bring themselves to take Mari away from her.

"Very touching," Father whispered to Mother, wiping a tear from the corner of his eye. Mother nodded, and blew her own nose before she opened Mari's bedroom door and helped Mrs. Panacek tuck Mari up.

"Good night, Mrs. Panacek," Mother whispered, tiptoeing out.

"Good night, Mrs. Panacek," Father said, outside the door.

"Good night, Mrs. Panacek," Mari murmured, half asleep, clinging to Mrs. Panacek's hand.

"Well, I don't know!" muttered Father. "It's . . . it's. . . ."

He lost track of what he had been going to say, cleared his throat again and went off to bed too.

13

SOMEHOW or other Father managed to get time off the next morning, even though he had claimed the previous day that he couldn't possibly spare a single minute. Mari skipped school. Mother had promised to write Mr. Weissensteiner an absence note saying Mari had a bad cold, or was at an old auntie's funeral. Mrs. Panacek suggested saying she was returning a madwoman to the mental hospital, but Mother didn't think that sounded like a good idea.

So here they were, all four of them, outside a tall barred gate. It was red and had a notice on it saying WET PAINT. There was a smaller sign on the wall by the gate, which said: ALDER YARD PSYCHIATRIC HOSPITAL.

Mrs. Panacek was frightened. She was holding hands with Mother and Mari, clinging tight.

"Well, come along!" said Father.

"For goodness' sake!" said Mother, clicking her tongue; she did not like it when Father made himself out to be a great leader.

"Somebody has to go first," he said, and he went ahead.

"Look at your high heels!" said Mrs. Panacek admiringly. "Aren't they lovely?"

"What?" Father stopped short in the middle of the gravel path. "Can you see my heels?" He anxiously tugged down his trouser legs. "Have you had the water in the washing machine too hot, Rosi?" he asked dangerously.

"Dear me, maybe I have!" said Mother in comic despair.

"Come on, what's the matter?" Mari was getting impatient. Three old women came out of the big yellow building. They were all holding hands, and they were all rather oddly dressed.

"Are they friends of yours?" Mari asked Mrs. Panacek.

"Yes," said Mrs. Panacek, but the women passed her and she passed them as if they had never met in their lives.

"We've known each other a long time," said Mrs. Panacek.

"Funny," said Mari.

Mari, Mother, Father and Mrs. Panacek went into the building. Mrs. Panacek didn't like going in, but Mari's parents gently propelled her through the door, and she had to go first. After all, in a way this was *her* home.

The porter shot out of his room. "It's not visiting hours," he growled.

Father rocked up and down on his heels. "We aren't visiting anyone," he said firmly. "We're bringing back one of the patients in this hospital."

"Oh," said the porter. "Sit down," he said, pointing to the shabby sofa in the waiting room, which was already occupied by three patients. Then he went back into his glazed booth and phoned.

"It's all right. You can sit down," said Mrs. Panacek. "They won't bite. *He* certainly won't!"

He was a thin old man who sat crumpled up in a corner, apparently waiting for something.

"He's always expecting someone to come," said Mrs. Pan-acek. "Sit down, sit down!"

Mrs. Panacek's mouth had suddenly gone very dry. Mari could tell from the way she kept running her tongue over her lips to moisten them. Was she frightened? Hesitantly, Mari's parents sat down. Mari stayed beside Mrs. Panacek, holding her hand.

Mother dug her elbow into Father's ribs. "Good God!" she said, in tones of horror, staring, fascinated, at the picture on the wall. It showed a stag in the forest. The picture was rather faded. "How frightful," whispered Mother.

Mari had to suppress her laughter. Mother herself would never paint a picture like that!

"That's a stupid stag," Mari said to Mrs. Panacek.

"Oh, but he lives here," said Mrs. Panacek. "He's always been here, ever since I came, and you mustn't chase him away or he'll be sad."

"Nonsense," said Mari, shaking her head.

"Oh, it's true, really!"

A nurse came along and put her hand on Mrs. Panacek's shoulder. "Well, Grandma, here you are again," she said.

"Yes, here I am again," said Mrs. Panacek amiably.

Mother got to her feet. "You listen to me, Nurse! Mrs. Panacek is not your grandma, and you ought to be more polite to her. This is a bit much!"

The nurse's eyebrows shot up and she looked at Mother in some surprise, as much as to say: Who in the world is *this?* Reading her thoughts, Mrs. Panacek said, "This is my Mari's mother." She took Mari's hand again, very firmly, so that no one could take her away.

"Family?" asked the nurse briskly.

"I won't have you calling Mrs. Panacek 'Grandma'!" said Mother, taking no notice of the question.

"Never mind," said Mrs. Panacek, a little wearily. "Perhaps the nurse wishes she had a grandma. Do you wish you had a grandma, Sister Clara?"

"Yes—no—I mean, no!" said the bewildered nurse. She took Mrs. Panacek's free hand and tried to lead her away.

"No!" said Mrs. Panacek. "Mari must come too."

"No, no," said the nurse mechanically, in a voice that was used to giving pointless answers to pointless questions a hundred times a day. "That's against the rules."

"Just a minute. Where is the doctor who's treating Mrs. Panacek?" asked Father. "I want to see the doctor. Now!"

The porter looked up from the newspaper he was reading and shook his head. An old woman in a striped nightgown had been watching the argument, interested and bright-eyed. Suddenly she began to cry.

"Go back to your room, Elizabeth," Sister Clara told her. The old woman turned and went down a long corridor, very slowly, still crying.

Mother hunched her shoulders up; she felt cold.

"After all, Mrs. Panacek's been staying with us," said Father, "and we're bringing her back. You can't treat us or her like this! I want to speak to the doctor."

"And perhaps you expect a reward for finding her too," muttered Sister Clara cuttingly, but when Father snapped, "What was that?" she said, "Nothing. I'm afraid Dr. Gottschalk is busy just now."

Mari felt furious with the nurse. She would have liked to jump on her from a considerable height.

"She has a kind heart really," Mrs. Panacek informed them. "She's just overworked. There are so many difficult people here. That's right, isn't it, Sister Clara?"

The nurse sighed, and her expression softened a little. "Yes, well, we understand each other, don't we, Mrs. Panacek?" she said. She cleared her throat. "Now, if you'd like to sit down again, I'll see if I can possibly find the doctor."

"So that's how it is," muttered Mother crossly.

"This place is quite impossible," said Father. "Treating people as if they were still in nursery school."

"She has a hard time," said Mrs. Panacek, still standing up for the nurse, which thoroughly confused poor Father. Why did Mrs. Panacek, of all people, take the wretched woman's side?

"I'm sure Mrs. Panacek is right," Mother now agreed. Father swallowed. Yet again, everyone was against him.

"I read somewhere what a hard time psychiatric nurses have," Mother said. "No one wants that sort of job because it's so much work."

A tiny little figure, not much taller than Mari and wearing a white coat, came around the corner. "So you've brought Mrs. Panacek back?" said this little woman. She turned out to be Dr. Gottschalk. "Goodness, what a funny little mite!" chuckled Mother. Unintentionally, she spoke loud enough for Dr. Gottschalk to hear. Mari blushed for her mother, but Dr. Gottschalk smiled kindly.

Father was pleased to find himself facing such a small woman; in these circumstances he swelled up proudly like a rooster. Usually *he* was the funny little mite, and if Mother wanted to annoy him for some reason, she would call him Little Tich and hide his shoes.

"Yes, here I am, doctor," said Mrs. Panacek, in rather a small voice. "I didn't mean to give you any trouble."

"That's all right, Mrs. Panacek," said the funny little mite. "I'm sure you had good reasons." She added, "I'm medical superintendent of this hospital."

Father was so impressed he could barely contain himself, and began stammering as he introduced himself and his family. So small, and she was medical superintendent of a hospital!

Father began telling the story, and Dr. Gottschalk listened carefully. Now and then Mother interrupted him, correcting something he had said and putting an arm around his shoulders. He kept trying to shake the arm off; he always felt very unmasculine when she embraced him in public.

"And what about you?" Dr. Gottschalk asked Mari. They were almost on the same level.

"This is Mari, Mari!" said Mrs. Panacek, hugging her. "Can I show Mari my room, doctor?"

And before Dr. Gottschalk could answer, Mrs. Panacek had swept Mari off down the corridor, which seemed endless.

"Room 144," she said. "Mine is Room 144."

Mari turned around. Dr. Gottschalk was asking Mother and Father into her office. Mother gestured to Mari, indicating that she was to come back soon.

"Okay," called Mari, and then jumped because her voice echoed so loud in the tall old building with its yellow-painted walls and white doors.

Mrs. Panacek opened the door of Room 144. It was a white door like all the others. "Come in," she whispered to Mari over her shoulder. Following her in, Mari was curious to know what Mrs. Panacek's room would look like.

At first she was disappointed. It looked like a perfectly ordinary hospital room: yellowish, boring and not particularly cheerful. There were three beds in the room. The bedside lockers were made of pale yellow metal, and were rather scratched.

"Hello," said Mari shyly. Neither the fat old woman lying in bed by the door nor the thin old woman sitting in a chair by the window answered her.

Nor did Mrs. Panacek say anything to them. She made for her own bed and sat down on the smooth gray blanket over it. There was a doll on the blanket.

"This is where I live," she said, running her hand over the blanket as if to smooth it out.

Mari just stood there, at a loss. Mrs. Panacek pulled out the drawer of her locker with a metallic squeal. She began searching frantically about in the muddle of photographs, pencils, bits of paper and lumps of sugar inside. Mrs. Panacek collected lumps of sugar the way some people collect stamps. Warily, Mari sat down on the bed beside Mrs. Panacek. The bed itself was so tall that once she was sitting on it Mari's toes did not touch the floor, and she felt uncomfortable.

You couldn't talk out loud in this room, Mari decided. She would have to whisper, or maybe scream, to break the silence. She could hear the old woman in the bed breathing. Mrs. Panacek's own search was being conducted in almost total silence too.

"There it is!" said Mrs. Panacek suddenly, so loud that Mari jumped. At last she put the packet of bubble bath samples which she had been clutching all this time down on the bed. Neither of the other two women in the room moved. Hadn't they even heard Mrs. Panacek?

"What?" said Mari, taking the photograph from Mrs. Panacek's hand. It was of a little girl with a teddy bear.

"My granddaughter," said Mrs. Panacek. She took the photograph away from Mari again, pressed it to her heart and began rocking to and fro. "So the murderer hasn't been back—oh, he would have been looking for the photo that time he came, the picture of my granddaughter! That's my *other* granddaughter. He's afraid, you see, because of the inheritance, but he has it all already, so I . . ." Mrs. Panacek lost the thread of her remarks.

Mari realized that she had not actually been listening to what Mrs. Panacek was saying. "Yes, of course," she said, and that satisfied Mrs. Panacek.

Mari could not help staring at the old woman by the

window, who was constantly staring out and looked as if she weren't alive at all. She looks stuffed, thought Mari, like the bear in the museum.

"What's the matter with her?" Mari plucked at Mrs. Panacek's dress—Mother's dress.

"Nothing, nothing." Mrs. Panacek was still rocking happily to and fro with the photograph in her arms and smiling. "She's waiting for her daughter," she said.

"Oh, is it visiting time now?" asked Mari, rather relieved to be given an explanation for the rigid way the old lady sat there.

"I don't know," said Mrs. Panacek vaguely. "She always sits there like that. Ever since her daughter died."

"You mean she's waiting for her dead daughter?" asked Mari, horrified.

"Maybe she isn't dead." Mrs. Panacek shrugged her shoulders.

"Don't you know for certain?"

"Oh, yes, she's dead. The daughter. A car ran over her; it's a long time ago now. Mrs. Borkovski sets the table for her every Sunday."

"That table?" Mari looked at the wobbly little wooden table in the corner. It had seen better days.

Mrs. Panacek nodded. "Every Sunday," she said. "I bring her coffee from Embacher's Delicatessen. The nurse makes it for us, and sometimes Mrs. Borkovski buys cake too, walnut cake, because her daughter was so fond of walnut cake, and then we eat all the cake up because her daughter doesn't come."

Mrs. Borkovski, the woman at the window, moved. "Is it Sunday?" she asked without moving her lips.

"No," said Mrs. Panacek.

"It'll be Sunday the day after tomorrow," said Mari. She got off the bed and went over to shake hands with Mrs. Borkovski. "My name's Mari," she said, offering her hand.

Mrs. Borkovski did not take it. She looked through Mari as if she were not there at all, shook her head sadly, and very slowly turned it to the window again. Mari shivered; she felt the prick of tears in her eyes. It was so awful to see Mrs. Borkovski sitting there sadly, not seeing anyone, not hearing anyone, just waiting for her daughter.

"Ah, she's off again," remarked Mrs. Panacek. "She's with her daughter now."

Mrs. Borkovski did not change her position, but her face lit up. She closed her eyes and moved her lips without uttering a sound.

"She's all right now," said Mrs. Panacek, beginning to take off her shoes and stockings.

Mari leaned against the wall and watched Mrs. Panacek putting her two odd stockings carefully on the bed, one of them red and the other black, and then rubbing her bare feet.

"Home again," she said. "Oh, I'm tired."

Mari went over to Mrs. Panacek. Suddenly she badly wanted to hug her. She did hug her. "Mrs. Panacek. I'm going now," she said. "But I'll be back, I promise."

"Yes," said Mrs. Panacek. She started to lie down on the bed, grunting a little.

"I really do promise to come back," Mari assured her again. She was a little disappointed that Mrs. Panacek didn't seem to mind her going. Somehow, Mari had rather hoped Mrs. Panacek would cry and feel very sad.

Instead, however, Mrs. Panacek repeated, "This is where I live," turned peacefully over on her side and closed her eyes.

"Well then, I'm going now," Mari said again.

Mrs. Panacek did not reopen her eyes. Mari backed to the door on tiptoe. She couldn't help it; tears were running down her cheeks.

"Go away, Heinrich," muttered the fat woman in the bed, opening her eyes. "Go away, Heinrich." She sighed and closed her eyes again.

Mari gave herself a little shake and went out of the room.

She felt better once she was in the corridor. She began to run to Dr. Gottschalk's office, where her parents were. Just as she was about to knock they came out.

"Everything all right?" asked Father, putting an arm around her shoulders.

"She's asleep," said Mari.

Dr. Gottschalk smiled. "She must be tired."

Mother said nothing, but rubbed noses quickly with Mari. "Now let's go and have some ice cream," she said.

"Yes, let's," said Father.

"Great!" said Mari.

"Good-bye, Dr. Gottschalk," said her parents.

"Nice woman," remarked Father, starting the car and putting it into reverse. "So small but so successful!"

"And kind regards from the transmission!" said Mother grimly, putting her hands over her ears.

"Well, we can breathe more freely here!" Father wound down the window and took deep breaths of polluted city air. Mother nodded.

"There's a café over there!" Mari bounced up and down in the back seat.

"Have anything you like," said Father grandly, giving the pretty waitress a big smile. Mother cleared her throat and said sharply, "This one's on me, dear." She was pleased when Father straightened his tie and cleared his throat loudly in annoyance.

And then they both smiled.

"Mrs. Panacek," said Mother later, eating her ice cream, "well, you know, Mrs. Panacek is . . . well, she's. . . ."

"Right round the bend!" said Mari.

"Yes, but kind of sweet; don't you think?" Mother looked helplessly at her melting raspberry ice cream, and started crunching a wafer.

"What do we do about her now?" asked Father.

"About Mrs. Panacek?" asked Mari. "Well, I did say I'd go back and see her."

Mother said, "Dr. Gottschalk told us a lot of the patients do get visited by their families, but Mrs. Panacek's only visitor is the murderer."

"He isn't a murderer," Father reproved her.

"No, but you know who I mean," said Mother lightly. "Her son-in-law, the one she's so scared of." A drop of ice cream fell on Mother's right shoe. "I wonder if she'd like it if we made her one of *our* family, so to speak? We could take her out once a month—go on expeditions with her."

"Good idea," said Mari happily, picking up her ice-cream dish to drink the dregs of liquid in it. "Good idea."

"Granny will hate it," said Father, frowning slightly.

"Who cares?" Shrugging her shoulders, Mother waved the absent Granny away. "Granny's behavior was nothing to write home about!"

"Right, we'll take Mrs. Panacek out from the Home every month," said Father, very pleased with himself, as if it had all been his own idea. "The bill, please!"

Out in the street, on the way to the car, Mari began to walk a tightrope without any rope.

"Come on, Mother, you do it," she said. Mother spread out her arms and followed Mari, laughing. A few people turned to stare. "You too, Father! I did this with Mrs. Panacek once."

Father shook his head uncertainly, then grinned and warily raised his arms a little way.

"You *do* look silly!" Mari shouted back over her shoulder.

"Silly brat!" Father shouted back cheerfully, and he be-

gan to run, arms flung wide. He put his right arm around
Mother, who was still tightrope walking, and his left arm
around Mari, pulling her toward him, and they all ran to the
car, laughing.

The people were still staring at them, shaking their heads.

"Hurry up, Mari!" Mother pulled the front of her bathrobe
together. "You're late again!"

Mari had overslept. It was ten to eight. She stood in her
room with nothing on, searching through her chest of draw-
ers. A clean undershirt flew to the rug, followed by a pair of
pants. Now for socks.

Mari looked at the socks and hesitated. She quickly put
on her undershirt and pants, and then stuffed the pair of
socks back in the drawer, looking around warily to make sure
Mother wasn't watching. She fished a red sock out of the
drawer. And then a black one.

Good. Mari put the odd socks on and looked at her feet,
pleased.

She heard footsteps coming closer.

"Do hurry up," said Mother crossly. "For goodness' sake,
get a move on, you lazy thing!"

Mari hastily buttoned up her blouse and pulled her jeans
on. Right. Now her shoes.

Were the jeans long enough? Mari looked carefully down
at herself.

Yes, they were. It was not until she sat down that you
could see she was wearing odd socks.

Quick, now for the bus!